SKIN DOMINION

SKIN HUNTER BOOK 3

TANIA HUTLEY

ONE

"You need to become President Morelle," repeats Sentin.

I sit gingerly back on my haunches and flick my tail from side to side, trying to wrap my mind around what he's suggesting. I'm in pain, and the thought of becoming the President of Triton makes my head swim.

We're in Felicity's bedroom, at the top of the Morelle Corporation building. Though Sentin's not as badly injured as I am, he's favoring one leg, and blood has dulled the shine of his Reptile Skin's jewel-green scales.

"Why me?" I demand. "Why don't *you* use Morelle's Skin?"

He blinks slowly, his eyelids coming up from underneath. "I had intended to. But I couldn't bring my human body up to the apartment. Your body is here, so I can re-code your chip."

My gaze drops to my battered human body lying on the floor next to President Morelle's Skin. The window's broken, and the curtains are billowing in the howling wind. Shards of glass litter the bloodstained floor around my body.

How did it come to this? All I ever wanted was to get my Leopard Skin back.

Okay, so that's not entirely true. What I really wanted was to stop Morelle from destroying my family. But I also took back my Leopard Skin, and even though I've been shot in the chest and flank, and I'm in agony, I'm not ready to give it up.

"If I transfer into President Morelle's Skin, I'll rule Triton." I say it out loud to hear how it sounds.

"You'll only be the *acting* president," he corrects. "And you need to transfer into the Skin quickly, so you can order her soldiers to stand down. Otherwise, they'll come up here and kill you."

I flatten my ears, staring down at the two bodies lying side by side. President Morelle's Skin couldn't be more different to my human body. I look like I urgently need a team of doctors to keep me alive, while the worst damage Morelle's Skin suffered in our fight was a torn blouse and a cut in its side.

"I need a minute to think," I tell Sentin.

"We don't have time." The scanner is in his long reptilian fingers, and he's holding it too close to my human body for comfort. One pass over my neck with that thing, and he'll wipe my chip and send my consciousness back into my body.

"One minute," I insist.

As though to emphasize how short of time we really are, a loud grinding noise and vibration comes from under my paws. Sentin disabled the elevator which is the only way up to the penthouse apartment, and now the president's soldiers are working on breaking through the floor. It sounds like they're getting close.

I let out a huff of breath that turns into a growl. "I'm just a grunt from Old Triton. I don't sound like Morelle. How can I act like her?"

"It won't occur to anyone to suspect anything. When you pretended to be Rayne, everyone believed you, didn't they? People see what they expect."

"And once we're safely out of here?" I ask. "You'll transfer into the Skin yourself, and I'll get my Leopard Skin back?"

"I need to remain in my own body. There are things Sentin can do that President Morelle can't." His tone is as calm as ever, but a ripple of color runs over his scales—the only sign he may be more impatient than he pretends.

"What things?"

"Our priority must be to negotiate peace with Deiterra. I'm the only one the imperator will talk to."

Seems that Sentin has a clear plan for what comes next.

Yes, of course he does. While I'm reeling from a suggestion I hadn't even considered, he has the future all mapped out.

In spite of the pain that goes with every movement, I push myself to all four paws and turn away from the twisted tangle of broken limbs that is my human body. I need to start coming up with my own plans. My reluctance to give up my Leopard Skin is clouding my thinking. What about all the things I could do if I become President Morelle?

"If I'm the president, I'll be able to help Ma," I say slowly. "And not just Ma. Tori, and Spade, and Keren, too. As President Morelle, I could make the lives of every sinker better."

His scales ripple again, growing darker. "I should warn you, the Skin might change you. Using it will give you a heightened sense of power. You could become more confident. Perhaps reckless. Even narcissistic."

I don't know what 'narcissistic' means, but becoming more confident doesn't sound like a bad thing. And power is something I've never dreamed of having. Especially power that'll keep the people I love safe forever.

Giving up my Leopard Skin was one of the worst things I could imagine, but all at once, it doesn't seem too much to ask.

"Guess we'll have to take the chance I won't go power crazy." I move back to my human body before lowering myself gingerly onto my belly. In the lab, I used to stay on four paws when transferring back into my own body. But I hurt so badly, lying down is a relief.

"You're ready?" Sentin crouches beside my head.

I drag in a breath, wishing I had more time to think this through.

"Where's Felicity?" I ask. "If she thinks Morelle's Skin is her sister, she shouldn't see it looking dead. Or coming back to life."

"She's still hiding in the secret room. All this noise must be frightening her."

Sentin shifts my human arm, and I wince at the unnatural way it moves. My bones are clearly broken, and the scent of blood is so strong, it's all I can smell.

"The damage to your body is severe, and I have no anaesthetic or pain relief to offer." Sentin's reptilian face shows no expression, but his tone is grim. "When I wipe your chip, you'll be jerked back into your human body. I'll re-code the chip as quickly as I can, but you'll have to bear the pain until you can transfer into the President's Skin." He lifts my human head and cradles it with one hand, readying the scanner.

"Wait. I need another minute." This is all happening so fast, and who knows when I'll get to be the leopard again?

"We're out of time."

I'm opening my mouth to tell him to give me another damn minute when my consciousness lurches sideways, slamming back into my human body so fast, I feel like I've fallen over and hit the floor.

Agony sears through me. Every cell of my body lights up with unbearable pain. My limbs are on fire. I open my mouth to scream, but there's no air in my lungs. If I manage to make a sound, I can't hear it over the pounding in my ears.

"Transfer!" Sentin must be shouting in my ear, but the sound is distant, muffled by the roar in my head. "Transfer now."

It takes everything I have to focus on what he wants me to do. Somehow I manage to close my eyes and force my mind sideways again, fighting my way out of the pain, searching for the President's Skin.

I find it.

At first, all I feel is relief that the pain has stopped. Then, in an exhilarating rush, other sensations hit me.

I'm so full of energy, I want to bounce to my feet. Instead, I ease up to sitting. I'm wearing a blouse with a small tear in the front, and a tight, long skirt. I can't even feel the cut on my side. My skin is the colour of mahogany, as richly bronzed as any New Tritoner. I bring up one hand, flexing my fingers. I'm used to having hands that are covered with calluses and the marks left by years of hard labor. Morelle's fingers are long and smooth, tipped with perfectly-groomed nails painted with a clear, shiny coating. And when I put my hand to my face, my fingers glide over a silky cheek instead of twisted scar tissue.

"How do you feel?" asks Sentin.

I look up at the Reptile Skin standing over me. His

scales have turned deep green. I can make out every smear of blood that mars their color, and detect the way his breath catches slightly on his exhalation, as though it hurts him to breathe. My vision is so sharp, it's even better than when I was the leopard. Every detail stands out so clearly, it's overwhelming. My brain can barely process it all.

"Milla, how do you feel?" repeats Sentin.

"Powerful." The word comes out in Morelle's voice, cold and authoritative. This Skin must have a voice synthesiser, because I sound exactly like her.

"Better than your Leopard Skin?"

Instead of answering, I push myself to my feet, the movement so easy it seems as graceful as running water. My veins could be filled with rocket fuel instead of blood. I'm acutely aware of the way my muscles tighten and release when I flex them. This Skin is incredible. If I wanted to, I bet I could punch right through the floor.

As the leopard, I was strong. Now I'm even stronger.

The feeling's intoxicating. No wonder Edward Morelle believed he could rule the world.

Sentin turns and limps out of Felicity's bedroom. I follow him through her toy room and into the hallway, where the floor is littered with deactivated Knight Skins, their chips ruptured with Sentin's sonic pulse weapon. My long, fitted skirt means I can only take short steps, but even the simple act of walking feels good, especially in bare feet. I spot Morelle's high-heeled shoes, which must have fallen off when Sentin carried this Skin into Felicity's bedroom. Though I stop to pick them up, I follow him into the living room without putting them on.

Sentin stops once we're well away from the dead knights. "Use your band and tell the soldiers to stand down," he says. "It has a thought interface like a mind pad, or you can control it manually."

I run my fingers over the delicate gold band on my wrist. It's finer than any band I've ever seen, with an intricate design etched into it. I have no idea how to use the thought interface, so I touch the sensor. When the control panel comes up, the number of apps it shows is dizzying. Is there anything this band can't do?

"There." Sentin extends his long forefinger. "Switch it to broadcast settings so I can interact with it."

I select the option he points to, and a 3-D projection of a Knight Skin appears above my band. The knight has a cat's pointed ears, an animal's snout, and is covered with black armor.

The knight salutes. "Yes, President Morelle?" It has a woman's voice.

Before I can speak, Sentin leans in. "The emergency is over." His tone is clipped and authoritative. "Order has been restored. Call your men back to their posts."

The knight salutes again, its yellow eyes unblinking. "Yes, sir."

That's right. I'd forgotten that the knights answer to Sentin as well as President Morelle. Edward Morelle must have trusted him to give him so much authority.

"One more thing," I say to the knight.

"Yes, Madam President?"

I open my mouth to give an order, then hesitate as the magnitude of the moment ploughs into me. I'm *President Morelle*. I have an entire army loyal to me. I could tell the knight to do anything at all, and she'd rush to do my bidding.

What if I ordered her to take all the floaters down to Old Triton to fill the shelters, and bring all the sinkers up from the darkness to move into their sun-filled mansions? Could I change the world with one command?

While I'm still hesitating, Sentin speaks up. "There's a girl here who requires urgent medical attention." He catches my gaze, and I realize he's talking about my battered human body.

I nod, quelling the urge to do something momentous. There'll be time once the current situation is cleaned up.

"I want repairs to the elevator started immediately," I tell the soldier. "Send a doctor to this floor as soon as you can get access to it." My Leopard Skin needs treatment too, but it can wait.

"Yes, Madam President."

After running and hiding for so long, being able to give orders feels like an impossible luxury, too good to last. "And another thing," I add, wanting to make the most of it. "Find William Scully. He's a soldier in my army. I want him back in his real body. He's not to transfer into a Knight Skin again. Bring him here, unharmed."

"Not up here," murmurs Sentin.

He's right, we can't start letting people into this apartment. Not with Felicity here.

"Take him to..." I hesitate, glancing at Sentin for guidance.

"There are bedrooms on level four."

That's a good idea. We lived on level four when we were training to compete in the Skin Hunter contest, and William will be comfortable in those rooms until I'm ready to see him. If I'm *ever* ready to see him.

For years, Ma and I talked about how much we wanted to find my brother and be a family again. But after watching William murder Doctor Gregory, that dream has soured. I owe it to Ma to keep him safe, but I don't think I'll ever be able to forgive him.

I give the order, then dismiss the knight. Uncertainty is whispering through me again, because not knowing where to take William has reminded me there's a lot I don't know yet, but it's a quiet voice in the back of my mind. Mostly, there's a fire burning through my veins. All the things that are wrong and unfair in Triton can finally change. *I* can change them.

The room has gone silent. The sounds from the apartment below have stopped, which means the soldiers have stopped trying to break through the floor. The knight believed I was President Morelle.

Sentin was right, I can do this.

I'm still holding Morelle's high-heeled shoes. I've never in my life worn a pair, but maybe this Skin will have muscle memory to guide me.

Easing my feet into the shoes, I wobble to the largest living room window, the one designed to catch and frame the most impressive view. Once there, I lift one hand and press it against the glass.

The Morelle scraper is so tall, we're almost in the clouds. The sun is close enough to look like it might brush the top of the building as it goes by. I'm closer to it than I've ever been, but this Skin's eyes must automatically adjust to the brightness outside, because I don't need to squint.

The view over New Triton is dizzying. I glimpsed it before, but now I have more time to look. And my eyes immediately go to the swathes of green on the other side of the wall. The green fields of Deiterra. I never imagined there'd be so much land not filled with buildings. It's both completely shocking and outrageously beautiful.

There are some buildings in the distance. From this

height it's difficult to tell how tall they are, but they don't seem even as high as Old Triton.

"Are the Deiterrans farmers?" I ask Sentin. "Do they grow their own food? No food factories needed?"

Sentin's silent for a few moments, as though he's reluctant to talk about Deiterra even though it's laid out in front of us. Then he inclines his head. "They haven't needed to manufacture food, although the war has taken its toll."

Smoke rises in the far distance, like a fire is burning, but the expanse of green in front of the wall is what draws my gaze. The fields are sectioned off, with different colors of green in different areas. Different plants, I suppose. Near the breach in the wall, some incredibly tall trees are stretching their branches to the sun.

"How much damage has been done by the war?" I ask.

"That's a conversation for later."

I glance back at the smoke. Could there still be knights in Deiterra? Is that where the war's raging?

Edward Morelle must have gazed out at this view every day for years. On this side of the wall, scrapers fill the city, bristling into the sky like a forest of sleek silver trees. But on the other side is all that empty space. No wonder Edward wanted to unite the two countries. If Triton could expand into Deiterra...

The thought fills me with air, like endless possibilities have just opened up in front of me and I'm about to take off and float through them. If the wall were to come down, Old Tritoners—my people—would have space and sunlight beyond their wildest dreams.

I can feel Sentin's gaze on me. He's studying me, his scales rippling with shades of blue and his head slightly tilted, as though he can tell what I'm thinking and doesn't like it one bit.

Reluctantly, I force myself to turn away from the window. I have a million questions about Deiterra, but now's not the time to ask. There'll be time later, though. I'll find out everything I want to know and decide what's best for Triton.

"I need to talk to Cale and make sure he's okay. And I need to check on Ma and Tori." With every word I utter, I realize it really will be as easy as that. I'm in charge. All I need to do is say what I want, and I can make it happen. My army will make it happen.

I can't wait for Cale to come up here and gaze over the green fields of Deiterra with me. We can make plans together. And I can give Ma and Tori all the things they've been dreaming of. Money. A home to live in. Safety and security.

My fingers go to the band on my wrist, running over the delicate circlet of gold. Edward's entire corporation now belongs to me. I own hundreds of factories and shelters, and I control the lives of millions of Tritoners.

I suck in a deep breath as a rush of exhilaration fills me.

My power is all but endless.

To change the world, all I need to do is command it.

TWO

"Can you heal it?" I ask the scientist.

My beautiful Leopard Skin is lying on its side on a gurney in front of me. Looking at all its wounds makes me wince. Large clumps of its thick fur are missing, and the fur that's left is matted with dried blood.

"Of course, Madam President. My team will work around the clock to ensure both the Leopard and the Reptile Skins are at full capacity as soon as possible."

I let out my breath. "Thank you."

We're in a lab room on the twenty-sixth floor of the Morelle scraper, in the Skin Research and Development division. I don't like this floor, because down the hall is the lab where the red-haired doctor was going to cut into my Skin so she could watch my human body bleed. Thankfully, this room isn't like that one. It has banks of computer screens taking up one wall, and cabinets full of equipment covering another.

Sentin is back in his human body. He wanted me to stay in the penthouse apartment so we could talk through endless details about the giant corporation I now own, but I needed to come here first, to make sure my Leopard Skin is in good hands.

"Seeing as we're doing such extensive repairs to the Leopard Skin, would you like us to upgrade it?" asks the scientist. He's been tweaked, of course, but the tightness around his eyes hints that he must be an old man. He has a slow way of speaking that reminds me a little of Sentin.

"What kind of upgrade?" I reach out to stroke a patch of unbloodied fur on my leopard's muzzle, resting my finger-tips against its soft fur.

The scientist rubs his chin, as though considering the options. "We can improve all aspects of the way it functions. But I assume you wish to keep the integrity of its form?"

"Are you asking if I want to change the way it looks?" My first reaction is to tell him no way. My Leopard Skin is the most beautiful creature I've ever seen, and he's asking if I mind him making it uglier?

On the other hand, if he can make my Skin stronger, wouldn't it be worth making changes? After all, my accident made me ugly, but that stopped mattering so much after I became stronger.

"Let me clarify." He pushes his hands into the pockets of his white coat. "Working on the Knight Skins, we perfected the integration of a ceramic composite with biological material. We can introduce a ceramic subcutaneous layer beneath the top epidermis, to render the Skin resistant to wounds such as the ones inflicted here."

"That was supposed to clarify it?"

He chuckles, as though he thinks I'm joking with him. "The introduction of a protective barrier will require us to remove the existing fur and skin before reintegrating it with

the new material. But we can perform the other enhance-
ments using non-invasive techniques."

I blink, trying to understand what he's saying. "You can
make the leopard bulletproof?"

"It won't be entirely bulletproof. But the new layer will
provide protection against all kinds of bladed weapons and
projectiles, including low-calibre ammunition. If you want
greater resistance, the thickness of the introduced ceramic
will need to increase, which may affect the Skin's
appearance."

Faced with the terrible wounds in front of me, how can
I say no? But even as I nod, I sink my fingers protectively
into my leopard's fur. "Do as much as you can."

"You'll be pleased, Madam President. I believe we can
exponentially increase the Skin's strength and endurance as
well. We've made significant advances in improving muscle
density and performance."

I run my fingers up to the top of my leopard's head.
Even there, patches of blood mar its beautiful, thick fur and
I have a powerful urge to pick the dried clumps out with my
fingers. But with the scientist's eyes on me, I shouldn't let
myself linger. Instead I turn away and leave the lab room.

The hallway I walk into is the one I ran down when I
was escaping this building. It was only a few days ago, and it
feels even more recent when I look through the glass doors
of lab rooms and see things I've glimpsed before.

In one lab is a pair of human legs wired up to a heart
floating in a large glass cylinder. In another, a metal animal
skeleton has a human face. A third holds a row of brains on
a long table, each with hundreds of needles bristling out
of it.

I don't go into any of those lab rooms to investigate what
kind of experiments the scientists are doing here, because

I'm not sure I want to know. But there is one room I stop in front of, and my heart beats faster as I look inside.

This is the room where Doctor James was going to slice me open. She's inside, bent over a small table, peering into a microscope. Her red hair is scraped back from her face just the way it was when she sliced into my leopard and I swore I'd kill her.

I push the door open. As I go in, she turns with a surprised expression. "President Morelle." She ducks a small bow, then extends her hand to shake mine. "It's a pleasure to see you. I've been hoping for a chance to tell you in person how sorry I am for losing the—"

"You're fired." I ignore her outstretched hand.

"Excuse me?" Her eyes widen and her hand drops.

"You're fired. Get your things and leave." I keep my tone brisk. Would I be taking so much satisfaction in doing this if I weren't in this Skin? It's impossible to know. But firing her feels surprisingly good.

"But... please, Madam President. Let me—"

"Leave now, or I'll have you thrown out."

Her mouth opens and closes, and the blood drains from her face, turning her cheeks gray. "May I know—?"

"No. Just leave." I step back and motion to the door.

She swallows hard, but walks to the door, hesitates, then goes out. I take one more look around the small lab room. Its antiseptic smell turns my stomach, but there's no trace of the gurney she had me tied to, or the scalpel she used to cut into me. I'm going to make sure nobody else ever gets carved up in here.

My band vibrates, and when I touch the sensor, the control panel that appears is still confusing. It takes me a moment to figure out how to accept the call, then the sharpest hologram I've ever seen appears above my band.

Sentin's human face is displayed in perfect 3-D, as though he's managed to poke his head through the control panel to talk to me.

"You're still on level twenty-six?" he asks. "Cale's here. I've granted him access to the penthouse."

"Thanks, I'll come up."

When I take the repaired elevator to the top floor, I find Cale staring out of the large living room window, gaping at the incredible view.

"Hey." I'm so relieved he's okay, I rush forward and throw my arms around him. But he stands stiffly, making the hug awkward, and after a moment I let go.

"You don't sound like Milla." He frowns at me, as though he thinks Edward Morelle might still be in the President's Skin, trying to trick him.

"The Skin makes my voice sound like this."

The lines in his forehead ease, and his wary expression relaxes. "You have an Old Triton accent."

"Have I? Hopefully nobody else has noticed." I speak more slowly, rounding my vowels and pronouncing every word. "Do I sound more like President Morelle now?"

He nods. "Is your human body okay?"

"Fine. The doctor patched it up, and now some high-tech machines are healing me."

My human body is in Edward Morelle's pod, the one he died in. I watched Sentin kill him in it, and now my body's lying there instead. I think that's creepy, but Sentin convinced me it was the safest place to keep my body, inside Edward's secret room behind a panel in the library, hooked up to all the machines that kept Edward alive for so long.

Sentin had Edward's body sent to the morgue without identification, and paid off anyone who might question how anybody could possibly live that long, or realize the most famous man in Triton must have faked his own death all those years ago. Even his ashes are now gone, scattered into the wind.

Funny to think that the man whose statue is in the middle of the central town square, and whose picture is in the lobby of all his factories, ended his days so anonymously.

"I can't believe we can see into Deiterra." Cale turns back to the window. "Look at all that green space. Is that farmland?"

"I think so." There's a heat haze shimmering the air, making the fields more difficult to see. But the enormous trees in front of the wall are still impressive, even from this height.

"New Triton looks so gray in comparison." He sucks in a deep breath and lets it out slowly. "This is crazy."

I don't know whether he's talking about being able to see into Deiterra, or about everything that's happened. Either way, he's right.

"I was worried about you," he says. "I didn't think you'd be able to climb this far up the outside of the building. There were too many knights to hold off for long, and I was afraid I hadn't given you enough of a head start."

"I couldn't have made it up here without you." I take his hand, threading my fingers through his. He's not as richly bronzed as I am, but his hands are as smooth and unscarred as mine. Twined together, our fingers seem to match for the first time.

But he grimaces and gently pulls his hand away. "It's too strange. I know it's you inside that Skin, but I can't look at it without seeing *her*."

"I understand." I let out a silent sigh. It's going to be hard to keep my distance. I used to hate being touched, but since the night we spent together in the safe house, I've been craving to feel his lips on mine again. Shame it's not going to happen while I'm using Morelle's Skin.

He stares back out the window, but his expression has changed and I can tell he's not thinking about Deiterra anymore. "It's brave of you to take on that Skin and everything that goes with it. But how long will you need to use it?"

I let out my breath, deciding how to answer. I don't blame him for hating this Skin after everything President Morelle put us through, but once he knows how much good I can do, he'll understand why it's necessary.

"Let's sit down and talk." I motion to the couch. "I'm not used to being in these shoes." Morelle's wardrobe is limited to high-heeled shoes and business suits. Edward Morelle used this Skin for years, but for some reason he doesn't even own a pair of jeans.

"How about you take the shoes off and we can talk while you show me around?" His tone is casual, but I can tell he doesn't want to sit close to me.

"It's me," I say. "I'm not Edward Morelle."

His mouth lifts in an apologetic half-smile. "Still."

His reaction to me now is so different to when we were in the safe house that a lump forms in my throat. But it's stupid to feel rejected. Kicking my shoes off is an excuse to turn away for a moment, to push my hurt feelings down where they won't show. And when I look up again, I can make myself sound casual. "Okay. I'll take you to see Felicity. This way." I lead him to the hallway.

"That's Edward's granddaughter, right?" When I glance back to him and raise my eyebrows, he adds, "Sentin told me."

"Where is Sentin?"

"He said he was going to your office."

"Did he?" No doubt Sentin's putting whatever schemes he has in motion. In a way, he's the one who has control of Triton now, though I still have final sign-off to any changes he wants to make.

"Felicity's been living here alone all these years?" asks Cale as we walk to her toy room.

"All her life. Edward stole her identity, so he couldn't let anyone know about her."

"And you're going to keep her up here?"

"It's all she knows. Would it be more cruel to leave her here, or to take it away from her?"

The door to Felicity's toy room is closed, and I knock before opening it. Felicity is sitting on a cushion on the floor in front of her dollhouse. "Poppa," she says with a flash of delight. Then her gaze goes to Cale and her smile drops away.

"Poppa is what she calls me," I murmur to Cale. "She's not used to seeing new people."

"Hello." Cale gives her one of his brilliant smiles. "I'm Cale. It's nice to meet you, Felicity."

She draws back. "Hello," she mumbles, turning her face away and hiding behind her long gray hair. She's sixty-four years old, but she's sitting on the floor with her legs tucked in beside her as though she were a child.

"It's okay, sweetie." I make my tone soothing. "Cale's a friend, and he'd like to see your dollhouse. Will you show him the people living inside it?"

As I step forward, I feel the breeze coming in through the broken window in Felicity's bedroom. Sentin said he's picked out a couple of loyal soldiers he trusts to come up to the apartment and fix all the damage we caused, including repairing the secret rooms that Edward Morelle built into the walls. But he wants to hide Felicity away while they work. I hate the thought of locking her in a room, but he's promised it won't be for long.

"Do you have a whole family living in your house?" Cale moves closer to Felicity, peering into her large doll-house as though he's fascinated by it. Inside, miniature people are walking around, performing the same tasks over and over. A mother rocks a small baby. A father endlessly stirs a pot on the stove. Two children chase each other around a miniature living room, and I've watched them for long enough to know they'll never catch each other. Now I'm over my initial wonder at the intricacy of her toys, they're actually a little depressing.

"They're *my* family." Felicity stares suspiciously up at him, as though he might be thinking of stealing the tiny robots.

"Of course they are. What are their names?"

As she tells him, she starts to relax. And when he keeps plying her with questions, her expression grows trusting. She's shoeless, and wearing baggy clothing. One of her full-sized humanoid robots is watching from the corner, sitting unnaturally still in a chair, with its hands folded in its lap. Her robots wash and dress her, feed her, and entertain her. Felicity isn't used to having real people around, but Cale has a natural charm.

"The little girl is Mellina, and she can run away," explains Felicity. "She can climb right up onto the shelf." She pulls the small doll out of its house and puts it on the floor. It immediately strides over to the large shelving unit against the wall, and starts climbing a miniature ladder. "Sometimes I tell her to dance with the others." On a higher shelf, Felicity has an entire troop of miniature robots that twirl and dance in an endless ballet performance. The small girl from the dollhouse climbs higher, seemingly determined to join them.

Cale glances at me, and I can read his expression as though his thoughts were printed across his face. For more than half a century, Felicity has been living a miniature life. She must have played with these toys more times than I can count, yet she's still absorbed with watching her dancers twirl in tiny circles. Her confinement has shrunk her world in more ways than one, and I can tell Cale finds that thought as disturbing as I do.

"I'll show Cale your bedroom," I tell her.

She nods, but stays where she is, staring fixedly at the little robot as it climbs the doll-sized ladder.

In Felicity's bedroom, the wind is blowing harder, whistling through the broken window. Felicity's robots have been hard at work. The blood and broken glass have been cleaned off the floor.

"This is where I crashed through the window to get in," I tell Cale. "The glass is thick enough that it would be hard for any normal person to break. But Sentin's going to have all the windows upgraded anyway so they're even thicker. So nobody can ever break in that way again."

Cale raises his eyebrows. "Is he expecting another leopard?"

"He said he wants to 'prepare for every eventuality'." I use the same words Sentin did, making quote marks with my fingers. "Having Felicity here makes him uneasy. He's paranoid somebody's going to find out about her."

"She can't sleep in here with the window broken," Cale points out.

"The new glass has to be specially made. In the meantime, there's another bedroom down the hall."

He nods, stepping forward to stare through the broken

window. The wind blows his scruffy black hair back, and the sun strikes his face, highlighting its sharp angles. His face is tweaked, designed to be perfect like everyone else in New Triton. Still, I can't stop staring at him. It's not just how handsome he is. It's because, if I look deeply enough, I can catch glimpses of his thoughts in his brown eyes.

Nothing about Cale is secretive. I always know where I stand with him, and usually it's one of my favorite things about him. But when he turns his gaze to me now, he's not looking at me like he usually does. He's looking at me as though I'm President Morelle, and the distance in his gaze makes my heart ache.

"Was it Sentin's plan all along for you to use that Skin?" he asks.

I swallow, taking a moment to make sure my voice sounds normal. "I think so. He said he can't be President Morelle, because he has to negotiate with Deiterra. The imperator will only talk to him."

Cale frowns. "Could he have meant for all this to happen? Predicted it, even before he entered the contest?"

"It sounds far fetched, doesn't it? But I really do believe he must have predicted some of it." Because Cale doesn't want me to touch him, I run my hand over Morelle's gold band instead, exploring the intricate patterns in the metal. As fancy as it is, it's a poor substitute for his touch.

Cale's gaze follows my fingers, his eyes troubled. "I asked you before how long you were planning to use that Skin. You didn't answer."

"As long as it takes to change things."

"What things are you going to change?"

I take a breath. Since transferring into Morelle's Skin, I've been thinking about little else, and I'm glad to have the chance to say it out loud.

"I'll start by restarting Sub Zero so the Fist can broad-cast again. And I'll destroy all the remaining Knight Skins. Then I'm going to find a way to make Old Triton safer, and give sinkers real homes instead of shelters. I'll pay them higher wages, and make factories better places to work." Talking about it makes my heart lift, and I find myself smiling at Cale. "It's hard to wrap my head around all the things I can do in this Skin. But it's exciting. It feels like I could work out a way to make the sun shine in Old Triton."

His expression lightens, some of his usual spark returning to his eyes. "If you can really do all that, it would make a big difference. The Fist have been trying to do those things for years."

"I *am* the Fist now."

"As long as it doesn't change you. Do you know what this Skin will do to your brain?"

"It's not going to do anything to my brain." I glance down at my bare feet, aware that I just lied to him. Then I meet his gaze. "Actually, Sentin said it might make me more confident. But that doesn't have to be a bad thing."

His frown comes back. "I don't like that it's going to do anything to you. It's not something you should take lightly."

"You think I should give the Skin to Sentin?" Though it's what I originally wanted, now the idea makes me feel ill at ease. "In this Skin I can make things better for Old Triton. If Sentin becomes President Morelle, what's to say he'll want to do the same? He doesn't care about Old Triton. Not like I do."

"Even with all the good things you can do, I'd rather have Milla back. That Skin has a coldness to it. I'm afraid it'll make you ruthless."

"If I get to give Ma and Tori a better life, it'll be worth it." He's still frowning, so I change the subject. "Speaking of

Tori, would you go and check on her? I'd do it myself, but if President Morelle turned up to the safe house, I'd probably start a gunfight."

"Shall I tell her what's happened, and that you have a new identity?"

"I guess so. But just her. As much as I like Spade and Keren, we can't trust too many people with a secret this big."

"What about your mother? And your brother?"

"I'd like to tell Ma." I step closer to the broken window, liking the fresh smell of the wind, and the way it buffets my face. "But I haven't decided what to do about William. I won't be able to look at him without thinking of Doctor Gregory." Even saying her name brings a lump to my throat.

"Milla." Cale hesitates for a moment, rubbing the back of his neck. "Do you think you can trust Sentin?" he asks finally.

"I don't really have a choice."

"There's something I want to tell you. When I was in the Knight Skin, you remember how certain I was that Sentin was on our side? I've been thinking about it, and I've realized the way I felt about him wasn't that different to the way I felt about Morelle."

I frown, trying to recall my own time in the Knight Skin. I don't remember thinking about Sentin at all while I was using it.

"The knights are loyal to Morelle because she wired those feelings into the Skins' brains," I say slowly.

"It sounds about as unlikely as him planning all this from the start, but do you think Sentin could have included himself in the knights' programming, and they're just as loyal to him?"

THREE

President Morelle's private office is on the floor below her apartment. It's huge, luxurious, and would take up the entire floor if it weren't for her assistant's office, which I have to walk through to get to it.

But I really need to stop thinking of Morelle's things as somebody else's. It's *my* office now, and her assistant works for me. Her name is Cassandra, and she's wearing a crisp, cream suit and an expression that suggests she's been doing this job a long time and can handle anything. She's as beautiful as any New Tritoner, but I'm starting to understand what Cale meant when he said he was tired of everyone looking the same. I suppose there are only so many ways you can configure your features when you're making them perfectly even.

"Good afternoon, Madam President." Cassandra stands politely as I walk through her office. "Sentin is waiting for you. I've forwarded the rest of your meeting requests and messages to your band, and prioritised them for your attention."

"Thanks." She seems so efficient, I'm a little afraid she'll see right through me. I keep walking and the door to my office opens automatically for me, its sensor probably triggered by my band.

My office has a giant boardroom table on one side that must seat at least thirty people. The windows are all opaque. They're cloudy white walls designed to let in filtered light and hide the view.

In fact, the only high windows that don't hide the view are the ones in President Morelle's private apartment. I guess she didn't want anyone else to see what's over the Deiterran wall.

Sentin is behind Morelle's desk—I mean, my desk—when I walk in. He's wearing a navy shirt and black jeans, and using the large holo screen to look at a whole lot of numbers.

"What's that?" I ask.

"Operational data for the Morelle Corporation." He frowns at it. "Prior to making any changes, it's important to analyze our revenue and expenses."

"Changes?" I move behind him so I can read the numbers. They all have lots of zeroes, and the totals are high enough to make my head spin.

He glances over his shoulder at me, his eyes sharp behind his high-tech glasses. "I assume you're here to talk about the changes you want to make?"

He's right, I am. I don't know how he does it, but I'm getting used to him being a step ahead.

"First, I have something to ask. I want to know about the Knight Skins, how they influence the thoughts of the people using them." I step to his side so I can see his gray eyes more clearly, though trying to tell what he's thinking is as impossible as making out the view through the opaque glass behind him.

Sentin makes the holo disappear, then swivels and sits back in his chair, stretching his long legs in front of him. "Have you noticed you speak differently in that Skin? Using the Leopard Skin changed your human body's physical capabilities. I wonder if this one is expanding your intellectual capacity?"

I blink, distracted. "You think this Skin's making me smarter?"

"The Skin's brain has its own neural pathways. It can cause your own mind to become more active in certain areas."

"Watch out, I might get smarter than you."

It's only a joke, but he answers seriously. "You've always had street smarts, Milla. That's something that can't be learned, except through experience."

"Wait. Did you just pay me a compliment?" I jerk back with my hand to my mouth, exaggerating my surprise to hide the fact that I'm actually flattered.

"Don't let it go to your head." He's as deadpan as ever, but I swear there's a glint of amusement in his eyes.

I'd take it further, but just because I'm joking with Sentin for the first time ever, I can't let myself get distracted. "Let's talk about the knights," I say, perching on the edge of the enormous desk.

He tilts his head back to look at me. "Go on."

"Morelle made sure the knights would be loyal to her. But they're loyal to you too, aren't they?"

"Yes, they are."

I blink at him. "But... how? Did Morelle know? And why did you do it?"

He's silent for a moment, as though considering my questions. Then he answers in the slow, precise way I've become used to. "I told you I assisted her scientists with some complex calculations in order to win her trust. The calculations were related to the way Skins can stimulate areas in the brain."

"You mean, you helped control her soldiers' minds?" My good feelings toward him disappear, and my voice rises. "How could you?"

He lifts both hands in a calming gesture. "I assisted with certain aspects of the technology. That answers your 'how' question. The answer to whether President Morelle knew the knights are loyal to me, is that she did not."

"I also asked why you did it. You weren't controlling them, were you? You didn't tell them to terrorize Old Tritoners and attack innocent people?"

The knights killed a lot of sinkers. If Sentin's to blame, I'll have to do something. Maybe order my guards to arrest him. But fighting Morelle together has made us a team, and even if I don't know whether I can trust him, I still think of him as a friend. Besides, I'm not sure I can pull off being the president without his help.

"I didn't give them any orders." His tone is as calm and as matter-of-fact as though we were talking about the weather. "My motivation for influencing the knights lies in the fundamental principles of probability theory. Although I calculate the most likely outcome of any event, the nature of predicted outcomes is that they may not necessarily occur."

I cross my arms. "What does that mean?"

"It means that I set a number of contingency plans in motion. Being able to command the knights may have become necessary. Fortunately, it didn't."

"You shouldn't have messed with those kids' brains."

"Noted." He waves at the chairs on the other side of the

desk. "Sit down, and we can talk through the changes you intend to make."

I puff out a frustrated breath. Arguing with Sentin reminds me of trying to handle magnetised vReal gel. I couldn't get a grip on that either.

"You know my brother is one of the kids you helped brainwash?" I demand.

He blinks slowly, giving nothing away, but clearly waiting for me to get to the topic he wants to discuss.

After a long moment, I let out another exasperated breath and ease off the desk, sinking into the chair opposite him instead. He's in the president's seat, and I'm in the one reserved for visitors, but I refuse to let that annoy me.

"I want to stop building new Knight Skins and destroy all the ones we have," I tell him.

Sentin links his fingers, his elbows on the arms of his chair. His palms tilt toward me and I notice a deep wound in the fleshy part of his hand, running all the way from his index finger to his pinky.

"The knights are under your command," he says. "It would be counter-productive to destroy them when you can simply order them to do your bidding. If they're doing things you don't like, just tell them not to."

"I don't want to order them to do anything," I say. "Not when they've had their free will taken away."

"The conditioning has already happened. You can't reverse it."

"I won't use those kids like Morelle did."

"If the soldiers have no Skins, they'll lose their sense of purpose. Consider how you felt when you were forced to give up your Leopard Skin. There are over a thousand young people who'll feel the same way."

If Sentin would lose his temper, he'd be easier to argue

with. But it's impossible not to doubt myself when he's always so damn logical.

I shake my head. "I won't let you talk me out of this. I know what's right and wrong, even if you don't."

"Most of the Knight Skins have already been destroyed by the Fist." Ignoring my barb, he pulls up some numbers on the holo screen. "Only forty-seven remain. Even if you insist on halting the production of new Skins, you must retain the few you have. They'll be necessary for our visit to Deiterra."

"Our what?" The green fields I saw from the window flash into my mind, and my heart speeds up.

"We're still officially at war. I've opened a line of communication with the Deiterran imperator to resolve the issues between us, and we must meet him face-to-face."

"In Deiterra?"

He nods, and I catch my breath.

The thought of getting to walk through those fields makes me dizzy. But meeting with the imperator and having the responsibility for stopping the war rest on my shoulders? That's not so appealing.

"What about your father?" I ask. "He's the ambassador. Can't he meet with the imperator?"

"My father was killed in the bombings."

I rock back in my chair, shocked by his matter-of-fact tone. "I'm sorry, Sentin. I didn't know."

"It happened while you were unconscious. I didn't expect you to know."

"I'm still sorry."

He gives me a nod. "Thank you." His gaze flicks down to the desk and his eyes cloud over. For just a moment, I catch a flicker of pain that's both raw and deep. Then he turns his face away, pushing his glasses further up his nose.

My heart contracts. Sentin isn't emotionless after all.

He clears his throat, and when he looks back at me, his armor is locked back into place. "Our priority must be to negotiate the terms of a peace treaty. We'll need to take the remaining knights with us to Deiterra, both to ensure your safety, and to create a presence that will help the imperator decide it's in his best interests to be reasonable."

I nod, resisting the urge to tell him it's okay to grieve. It hasn't been that long since the bombs went off, but Sentin's better at hiding his feelings than anyone I've ever met. If he wants to pretend he has no heart, that's up to him. At least I finally know the truth.

"I missed quite a lot of the war," I say instead, with a casual shrug. "Were we winning?"

"Our knights came close to defeating the Deiterran army. If the Fist hadn't wiped the chips of most of our soldiers, the imperator's regime would have fallen by now."

"Really?" I gaze up at the ceiling to give myself time to think. There's so much to do here, I'm reluctant to leave. On the other hand, I never dreamed I'd get to go to Deiterra.

Funny to think that if I'd waited a few days before breaking into the Meat Locker to rescue William, or if I hadn't wiped all those soldier's chips, I might now be the interim president in charge of Deiterra as well as Triton.

"Can I travel in this Skin?" I lift both hands, as though showing him my palms will somehow help him answer my question. "My human body is being fed with tubes, right? And this body seems to be working like a real one. I've been testing it. So far, everything works like a real body. I've been eating and sleeping, and... doing everything else a real person would."

His lips twitch. He knows what I mean by 'everything

else' without me having to spell out how I nervous I was the first time this Skin needed the bathroom.

"Your Skin was created from Felicity's DNA," he says. "It has identical biological functions, and you need to fuel the Skin with food, just as she fuels her human body. The only modification is its ceramic composite skeleton, and fiber-optics that mimic the function of a spinal cord."

"But it's stronger and faster than a human would be."

He inclines his head. "It was grown under laboratory conditions, so those traits were easy to enhance. But although the scientists improved on nature, genetically speaking, your Skin is a copy of the real Felicity. The only reason you don't look more like her is because the Skin reflects a tweaked version of her, to fit with New Triton norms."

"And if I take it to Deiterra, being such a long way from my human body won't matter?"

He shakes his head. "The technology uses quantum entanglement. A close proximity is required for the initial consciousness transferal, but subsequent communication is instantaneous, and distance becomes irrelevant." He blinks at me, probably registering my blank expression. "Just be aware that if you transfer out of the Skin, you won't be able to use it again. It will appear to be unconscious until you get close enough to transfer back into it and resume control."

"Okay." I make up my mind. "Let's go to Deiterra, and I'll wait until we get back before I destroy the last of the Knight Skins. But before we go, I want to help the people of Old Triton. I'll start by increasing the amount they get paid for working in my factories."

He blinks slowly, and I can almost see the cogs spinning in his brain.

"You have over a million employees," he says after a

moment. "Lifting wages across the board will be prohibitively expensive."

I gesture to the deactivated holo mechanism on the desk. "You were looking at some big numbers when I came in. The profit column looked particularly impressive."

"If you bankrupt your company, your employees will have no jobs at all."

Restlessly, I get up from my chair and pace to the opaque windows, still a little wobbly in the high heels I haven't quite gotten used to.

"You've analyzed the numbers, right? How much of an increase can I afford to give them?"

"That's not the only consideration." He swivels his chair to face me. "Everything in Triton is interconnected. You're part of a consortium of factory owners who work together to protect their mutual interests. They set wages to maximize their profits. Upsetting that balance will turn them against you."

I snort. "So Triton's factory owners are a group of sharks who like to steal from goldfish? I've seen that plenty of times, and they don't scare me like they used to."

He raises his eyebrows. "Goldfish? Stompers? You need to be careful not to use Old Triton slang when you're in that Skin."

Dammit, he's right.

"What if all the factory owners had to raise the wages they pay?" I speak slowly, making sure I pronounce each word like a New Tritoner would. "I could make it a law. As the acting president, I can increase the legal minimum wage, can't I?"

"The industrialist consortium is powerful. Its members will fight you."

I frown at him. "Of course the factory owners don't want to pay more. That's why it needs to be a law."

"The presidential election is in a few months. You should wait until you're officially elected."

"You want me to run for president?"

A crease appears in his smooth brow, which in Sentin-land means he's shocked I had to ask the question. "Of course."

It makes sense that Sentin wants me to hold onto power. But the election is almost a year away, and I can't let millions suffer in the meantime without trying to help.

"There must be some middle ground," I say. "We could give workers a small wage rise at first, with a plan for more after the election. Even a tiny increase will help. For some Old Tritoners, it could mean the difference between life and death." I have no idea if he cares about dying sinkers. "Besides," I add. "Won't giving them more money mean Old Tritoners will be more likely to vote for me?"

"Perhaps."

At least I'm making a little progress. "I also want to get rid of second child taxes, and make shelters safer for the grunts who have to live in them."

"Workers," he corrects. "Not grunts."

Silently cursing my slip, I keep going. "Eventually, I want to give them their own houses to live in, instead of shelters."

"Change always comes with a cost. I'd rather not have to pay it now."

"Old Tritoners *need* things to change. The longer we wait, the more they suffer."

He studies me for a moment, his eyes the color of steel. "Why are you so concerned with Old Triton? You don't live there anymore. You'll never need to live there again."

"You think I can just forget about everything that happened to me there?"

"You don't need to forget it. Analyze it, and learn from it. But holding onto old emotions and attachments will only weaken you."

I think of Tori, and the all the Fist members who went to battle, risking their lives against the knights. If they'd decided that emotions and attachments weren't worth fighting for, the knights would probably still be tormenting Old Tritoners.

"Is that what you do?" I ask. "Cut yourself off from everything?"

He rests his elbows on the arms of his chair and laces his fingers. "It's the only sensible option."

"How can you not care about anyone?"

He hesitates. "It's not that I don't care. But the fact is, a whole is greater than the sum of its parts."

"What does that mean?"

"I'm concerned with the community as a whole. The future of Triton matters far more than what happens to any single individual."

"That's great," I walk back to the desk. "Unless you're the individual who's getting shafted."

"Leaders can only be effective if they remain detached."

"Maybe that's true, but I'm not detached. Too many terrible things happen every day in Old Triton. Those things happened to *me*. I can't walk away and pretend I don't care."

He doesn't reply, and I stop in front of him, wishing for the millionth time that he were easier to read. Even sitting down, Sentin has a restrained elegance that probably comes from having such long limbs. His facial features aren't as even as most floaters', and I'm starting to think of that as a good thing. His dark hair is short, his eyes are sharply intelligent, and I recently discovered that on the rare occasion he smiles, the way his face lights up takes my breath away.

I can't help but like Sentin. But I'd give my right arm to know if I can trust him.

"You cut your hand?" I ask, noticing it again.

He lifts his palm to give me a good look. The wound is deep enough to make me wince. "When I collected the chip scanner from Felicity's bedroom, I cut myself on a piece of broken glass. My own impatience was to blame. I should have let her androids clean the room first."

So he's not infallible after all. Just a regular guy who occasionally makes mistakes, like the rest of us. I was starting to wonder. "Doctor Gregory said you studied military tactics at university," I say.

He inclines his head. "Military tactics, statistics, and probability theory. I have an aptitude for mathematics."

"I'm determined to make things better for Old Triton and could really use your talents. I don't want to have to do it without you." I shoot him a smile to take the edge off my words, but hopefully he can see how serious I am. He has no reason to want to improve conditions in Old Triton, but if I let him talk me out of it, it'll be on my conscience. I'll have to think about all the people I let suffer, when I could have pushed for change.

"That Skin gives you absolute power," says Sentin. "But now is when you must be most careful. You know what they say about power."

"I have no idea what people say about power. I never thought I'd have any."

Only a few short weeks ago, I was living in the shelter, solely worried about surviving. Everything changed the night I watched two shiny goldfish swim in out of the rain.

He blinks slowly. "Be careful, Milla. The changes you want to make will upset some powerful industrialists, and change Triton in ways you can't foresee."

Though a warning from Sentin isn't something I'd be wise to ignore, I nod calmly. "It's better than not changing things at all."

FOUR

Ma looks every bit as weary as the last time I saw her, and I have to clench my fists to keep myself from hugging her.

She stands stiffly in my luxurious private office, her forehead creased with confusion, and fear in her eyes. "You wanted to see me, President Morelle?" She's so overawed by the woman standing in front of her that her voice is barely more than a whisper. I wish I could tell her who I really am, but Sentin warned me against it and I figure I should follow his advice.

"I have something for you." I extend my arm, offering her my band.

It takes forever for her own arm to slowly extend. She looks as though she's expecting a trick, as though my band might contain some kind of deadly weapon.

I tap my band against hers, activating the transfer function. "I've just given you the key that will open your new home. The apartment's not large, but it's in New Triton. And it's all yours. Paid for. The only thing you need to do is move in."

"I don't understand." She frowns at her band, her arm still stiffly extended.

"Congratulations." I take her work-roughened hand in mine, and shake it for longer than I should because I can hardly bear to let it go.

But her hand stays limp in mine, and she looks at me with such wariness, I can't stand it. She won't pull away, she's too afraid of me for that. But she doesn't welcome my touch. And why should she? I'm the woman who owns the factory where she slaves for endless hours, and the shelter where she fears for her life each time she closes her eyes.

I drop her hand and clear my throat, trying to get rid of the lump that's formed. "I know it's a lot to take in, so let me say it again. You now own an apartment in New Triton."

Her frown deepens. "In New Triton?" She sounds as though I've suggested she relocate to Deiterra.

"It gets the sun," I say. "And your account has been filled with credits. You won't need to work, and if you have friends you'd like to see, you can go down to Old Triton any time you like. I mean, if you want to..."

My voice trails off. I'm the most powerful woman in Triton, but somehow I still feel like a girl trying to please her mother. I'd been looking forward to this meeting, to giving Ma a place of her own, but her confusion and fear is sapping all the pleasure out of it.

"Milla is safe," I say on impulse.

Her mouth drops open and her eyes light up. "What? Where is she?" Her voice finally strengthens to a normal volume.

"She's safe," I repeat. "She's helping me with something important, and agreed to go away for a while. I'm sorry I can't tell you any more than that. But you should see her again soon."

Ma draws in a breath and looks like she wants to press me with more questions, but caution wins out. After a moment she nods. "Thank you."

I nod back. Though I'd imagined how great it would feel to make Ma happy, I clearly haven't, and her gratitude doesn't feel good at all. It feels all wrong.

When I drop my gaze to the floor, searching for something to say to make this interview less painful for both of us, she takes it as a dismissal and starts backing toward the door.

I jerk my head up. "Wait. I need to ask you something."

She freezes, and her nervous expression makes me feel worse than ever.

"Your son, William," I say. "He knocked you out and left you for dead."

She nods, and her expression becomes pleading. "Do you know where he is?"

"He's here, in the building. I discharged him from the army."

"May I see him?"

"You've forgiven him?" My chest feels like something heavy is pressing down on it.

"Of course. He's my son."

The simplicity of her statement takes my breath away. Maybe I still have some love left for William too, but forgiveness won't come so easily.

"I'm going to issue him with new orders. I'll tell him to protect you, take care of you, and never hurt you again."

Her eyes widen. "Please don't do that."

"Why not?"

She swallows, clearly regretting speaking up. But after a moment, her chin lifts and her voice firms. "Loving someone and wanting to take care of them isn't something he should be commanded to do. I hope he doesn't want to hurt me anymore, but it needs to be up to him."

I press my lips together, tempted to give William the order anyway. If he hurts Ma again, I'll feel responsible. But after a moment, I give a reluctant nod. "All right. If you don't mind waiting for a few minutes, I'll send for him and you can both go."

I touch my band to summon Cassandra, and she leads Ma into the next room to wait.

Now comes the interview I've been dreading. I move behind my big desk and sink into the chair before letting Cassandra know I'm ready. "Bring him in," I tell her.

William marches into my private office like the obedient soldier he is. He stands to attention, his eyes fixed straight ahead. His eyes look hollow, as though he hasn't been sleeping.

With him in front of me, all I can think of is the way he murdered Doctor Gregory, then left me strapped to a chair to be examined and dissected.

Bile rises in my throat.

Though my brother isn't tweaked, he's naturally hand-some enough that he could almost pass for a New Tritoner. Ma used to be beautiful once, before all the hard work wore her down, and William has her generous lips and high cheekbones. But I'm struggling not to see him as a monster.

He stands stiffly in front of my desk, waiting for me to say something. If I don't talk, he'll probably stand there forever. He thinks I'm President Morelle, the person who tricked Ma into sending him to one of her academies, turned him against his family, and taught him to kill. The irony is how much he loves Morelle, and how much he'd hate me if he knew I were the one really sitting in front of him.

"At ease, soldier." My muscles are tight and I need to force myself to lean back in my chair so I don't look as tense as I feel.

William puts his arms behind his back at the command, but still stands ramrod straight. I could invite him to sit down, but I don't want to drag this out.

"The Knight Skins are no longer needed," I tell him. "I'm planning to wipe every soldier's chip and scrap the Skins."

William's eyes widen and he opens his mouth to protest. His feelings are plain, written into his face. Shock. Dismay. Loss. But he closes his mouth before speaking, his loyalty to Morelle keeping him silent. He stares at the wall above my head. Maybe he was taught to keep his chin up, or not to stare a superior in the eyes. It's a little disconcerting talking to him when he won't look at me, but it's making this meeting a little easier.

"I know that isn't what you want," I say. "Believe me, I understand how difficult it is to lose your Skin and go back to being what you were before. Weaker and slower, and *less* in every way. After you've been a knight, how can you bear to be only human again?"

His eyes finally flick to me, surprise overcoming his training. I guess he didn't expect me to express what he was feeling. But losing my Leopard Skin after the contest was so devastating, it left a mark I'll never forget.

"I taught you that the army was your family," I go on. "I told you your own family abandoned you. But that was a lie. I'm releasing you from service, so you can go back to them."

His jaw tightens and a sullen expression crosses his face.

"Speak," I order. "Tell me what's on your mind. And be honest."

"Please don't take away the knights, Madam President." His voice is strained. "They're all we have."

"You have families."

"We don't, ma'am." His gaze drops to me properly now, gauging my reaction to his outburst. He studies me for a moment, then softens his tone. "I mean, like you said, Madam President. The army is our family. Knights are who we are."

"Not any more."

"You said my family didn't deserve—"

"I told you things that weren't true, so I could break your connection to them and gain your loyalty. Your family only want the best for you."

"You sound like *her*. Like my sister." For a moment I'm sure he's guessed everything and knows who I am. But he lets out a sigh. "You sent me to kill her, Madam President, and I was ready to obey."

"I shouldn't have given that order."

"I wanted to kill her. I wanted to make her suffer, the way I suffered when I first went to the academy." He bows his head, his fists clenched by his side. But his eyes are still defiant. Still conflicted.

The words, 'I'm sorry', are on the tip of my tongue. But President Morelle wouldn't apologise to one of her soldiers.

"Your mother is here," I say instead, the announcement more abrupt than I'd intended.

He stiffens back into soldier stance, his back straight and his eyes snapping to the wall above my head. "Excuse me, Madam President?"

"I had your mother brought here. She's in the next room, waiting to see you."

"I don't want—" He breaks off, flushing. "I'm sorry,

Madam President, I mean, yes ma'am. I'll obey any command you give me, ma'am."

In spite of what Ma said, I can barely stop myself from ordering him to forgive her and love her again. Though it wouldn't be real, at least I'd be able to rest a little easier if I could be sure he wasn't going to hurt her.

"From now on, your choices are your own," I say instead, my tone harsh. Then I activate my band to talk to Cassandra. "Take Private Scully to see his mother."

She leads my brother to the room where Ma is waiting. The room has its windows and doors screened off so their meeting seems private, but I've already discovered that Edward Morelle hid cameras everywhere. When I activate the holo function on my band, it's like being in there with them.

Ma is sitting at the large table in the middle of the room when William walks in. Her 3-D holograph is so sharp, I catch every detail of her expression as it transforms with joy. She jumps out of her chair so quickly that she knocks it over and doesn't notice.

William's image is just as clear, but his expression is a lot harder to read. As Ma throws her arms around him, he stands stiffly with his arms by his sides, so she ends up hugging them against his body. She's shorter than he is, and when he looks down at her head crushed against his chest, he pulls his shoulder up until they're around his ears.

She hugs him so hard and for so long, I keep expecting William to react. To do something. But he just stands there, letting her hug him, until my throat is so tight it aches. I want to stride into the room and knock some sense into William's stubborn head. If only I could force him to understand how much Ma has given up for him.

Ma keeps hugging him for so long I can't bear it.

Slowly, painfully, William's shoulders drop, and his arms inch their way up until his hands settle on Ma's lower back. He lowers his head so his face is beside her hair. Then he's actually hugging her, and his face contorts. His eyes brim with tears.

The lump in my throat expands until it's so big it's choking me.

I switch off the holo, and the two figures vanish. Then I walk over to the opaque window and take a few deep breaths. I've done all I can. What happens next is up to them.

My band vibrates, and when I look down, I see Cassandra is calling. "Madam President, I'm sorry to disturb you. You have an urgent call. It's Hendrick."

"Hendrick?" I ask.

She hesitates, and I can hear her confusion in the length of her silence. Hendrick must be someone Morelle knows well.

"The Beast," she says eventually.

"Ah." I blink at my barely-there reflection in the opaque glass. I wonder if he's anything like the stories people tell about him. "Connect us," I tell Cassandra.

A man's face materializes from my band's holo display. He must be from New Triton, but he doesn't look like any floater I've ever seen. He's a lot bigger than most, with a meaty face and not a single hair on his head. Some sinkers are bald, but for a tweaked New Tritoner to have a shiny head means he must have designed it that way. He has no eyebrows either, and such a thick neck that his head seems to flow straight into his shoulders. He's the biggest meat-sack I've ever seen. Somebody who clearly doesn't want to look like other floaters.

The Beast is one of the powerful industrialists Sentin

was talking about, a billionaire who owns factories in Old Triton. He's a recluse who stays out of the public eye, and there are a lot of rumors about him. One of those rumors is that he really does look like a beast. That one seems mostly true. He's a huge, hairless beast who happens to wear a suit.

"Ed," he says, his voice deep and gravelly.

My heart stops. I jerk my face away from his image, faking a cough to cover my shock.

The Beast thinks I'm Edward Morelle? That means he knows this is a Skin.

He must have been a very good friend of Edward's if he knows his secrets. I'll need to be extra careful not to give myself away.

My instinct when I look back at him is to say the man's name or give him some kind of greeting, but whatever I say could be wrong. Instead I nod, trying to pretend I haven't quite recovered from my coughing fit.

"What the hell is going on?" he demands. "You want to raise the minimum wage?"

I nod again. "That's right."

"Is this some kind of joke?" When he frowns, his eyes sink into the fleshiness of his face. Without eyebrows, the expression looks odd.

"No joke."

"You think I still owe you something? I don't. So cut the shit, Ed, because I won't stand for it. Tell me what's going on."

"Wages in Old Triton are too low. The workers are suffering."

"So?" His frown deepens.

"It needs to change."

"What are you talking about?"

"Triton needs to change."

"You've lost your mind." His wide nostrils flare. "I won't let you ruin what I've built. If you carry on this way, our history is over. You hear me? You break our agreement, we'll come down hard. Are you ready to go to war with us? Is that what you want?" Spit flies from his mouth, vanishing as it reaches the edge of the hologram display.

I drag in a breath, fighting to keep my face expressionless. The rage in his voice makes me want to shift the projection away. His fury is so intense, it's like a physical attack. If I were really standing in front of him, I'd be bracing for him to take a swing at me.

"I don't want war, and I have no quarrel with you." With an effort, I keep my tone calm. "But I'm going to improve the conditions in Old Triton."

"Then you're starting a war."

"It's time the citizens of Old Triton had some—"

"I don't know what you're playing at, but believe me, we're not going to take it."

"We?"

"The others are with me on this, as you must have known they would be. This is your only warning, Ed. You just signed up for more trouble than you can handle." His face vanishes, the line disconnected.

I stare at the shimmer of my reflection in the window's opaque glass, and a woman I barely recognise stares back. I guess this was what Sentin meant about unintended consequences. Could this Skin have made me so overconfident, I've managed to stumble into serious danger? Problem is, I'm feeling my way through the dark, living a stranger's life, doing a job I know nothing about.

In fact, there's only one thing I'm feeling certain about right now, and it's that a war with the Beast is the last thing I need.

FIVE

"Do you want to see Ginger beg?" asks Felicity. "Watch this."

She makes a hand gesture and her dog gets on its haunches, waving its front paws in the air. It cocks its head and its tongue lolls out of its partly-open mouth. It always looks like it's smiling. Maybe real dogs do too, I'm not sure. I've only seen them on the holo.

"Clever," I say, trying to sound enthusiastic.

I'm in Felicity's toy room, sitting next to her on the floor with my high heels kicked off and my legs tucked under me. Morelle's business suits mostly have fitted skirts, but they've been annoying me so much, I've only been wearing the few that have trousers. Cassandra's organising some casual clothes and flat shoes. Maybe my change in wardrobe will make people suspicious, but I've been too uncomfortable to care.

"Ginger can talk." Felicity's eyes are bright. "Talk, Ginger."

The dog barks, wagging its tail.

Felicity beams at me proudly, as though she taught the

dog the trick instead of activating a pre-programmed command.

"Good dog." I force a distracted smile. I've been trying to spend as much time as I can with Felicity, but I can't stop worrying about the Beast, and Ma, and, well, everything.

"Hey." Cale appears at the door.

I asked him to meet me here, and I knew he was on his way up, because I had to activate the elevator for him. Still, my heart leaps to see him, and my forced smile turns into a real one.

"I like your dog," Cale says to Felicity. "What's his name?"

"Ginger. She's a girl. Want to see her talk? Talk, Ginger." Felicity looks delighted to see Cale. As old as she is, she'd probably never met anyone new before Cale and Sentin started showing up. I can't imagine how lonely it's been for her with just a bunch of robots to talk to.

If I weren't so busy, I'd spend more time with her. Sentin's been helping run the Morelle Corporation, but it's an enormous company. Cassandra's managed to shoulder me with a ton of small decisions about things I don't really understand, like production targets and supply chains. And there always seem to be dozens of people who want meetings I have to bluff my way through.

I push myself up off the floor. "I'm sorry, Felicity, but I need to talk to Cale now. I'll come back later, if I get time." Leaving my shoes off, I follow Cale to the living room where we sit together on the couch.

"Maybe I can find a better place for Felicity," I muse aloud. "A real home with real people."

"When I suggested it the other day, she seemed terrified of the idea. Moving her might cause more harm than good."

I let out a sigh. "All I've been hearing for the last few

days are reasons why I shouldn't change things. When I became President Morelle, I thought I'd be able to do anything. But nothing's that simple."

Cale shoots me a sympathetic look. "Has Sentin been holding you back? Where is he?"

"Organizing our trip to Deiterra." I raise my eyebrows at him. "Actually he's almost as busy as you," I say pointedly, because when I called Cale earlier, he was in a meeting with some other high-up Fist members, and couldn't talk to me. "Sounds like you're a big shot in the Fist now? Not that I'm surprised. You and Tori are cut from the same cloth."

Cale is probably the only member from New Triton the Fist has ever had. The fact he's made it to the top says a lot.

"Talking about Tori, I wanted to tell you the news in person." His expression has turned serious. "She went through the breach in the wall, and crossed into Deiterra."

"What?" A cold chill runs down my back. "Is she okay? Why would she do that?"

"You know some Fist members tried to get through and were killed? Well, after we managed to destroy so many Knight Skins, the breach wasn't so well guarded and she must have seen an opportunity to make it through. Instead of asking someone else to risk their life, she wanted to try for herself."

"Did she make it?" I turn my head to the large feature window, as though I'll somehow be able to spot her running through the distant green fields of Deiterra.

"We think so."

"Nobody's heard from her?"

He shakes his head. "She's not answering calls. But that doesn't mean anything." His voice is soft and his eyes are as light as I've ever seen them, full of sympathy. "I'm sure she'll be okay."

"What if she's not?" I chew my lip, feeling sick.

"You'll probably see her when you go to Deiterra, and she'll bore you with stories about how much she loves it over there, and what a great time she's been having."

Weaving my fingers together on my lap, I tell myself he's right. Tori's a survivor. If anyone can make it in an unknown land, it's her.

For the first time, my upcoming trip to Deiterra seems like a good idea. If she needs help, I'll be there.

"Will you come with me?" I ask. "Help me look for her?"

His eyes widen. "To Deiterra? Did Sentin say I could—?"

"Not everything's up to him." It comes out blunter than I mean it to, and I soften my tone. "I'm sorry. It's just frustrating."

"Sentin's making things that difficult?"

"He doesn't want me to make any changes until after the election, but I keep thinking about all the people I suffered with in the shelter. I've scaled back my plans to just a tiny wage increase and nothing else, and he's still reluctant."

He nods. "Those people need help. The sooner the better, at least, from their point of view."

"See, you agree with me because you've spent time in Old Triton. Sentin hasn't. As smart as he is, he has no idea what it's really like. If he'd slept even one night in a shelter, he'd be on my side."

"What if you don't change anything, and then lose the election? You'll have lost the opportunity."

"Exactly. But Sentin made it sound like an extra fifteen credits a day for workers was going to destroy the whole infrastructure of Triton." I realize I'm squeezing my hands too tightly, and force them apart. "And he's not the only one. Have you heard of a factory owner called the Beast?"

Cale frowns. "Sure. But I can't decide if he's a real person or an urban legend. I don't think he's ever let himself be shown on the holo."

"He's real, and the rumors about him are true. He called a couple of days ago, and he's as odd looking as everyone says."

"What did he want?"

"To warn me not to break the agreement he had with Edward Morelle. Then he called again last night to inform me he's not going to pay higher wages. He's pretty angry."

"He threatened you?" Cale leans toward me. For a moment I think he's going to put his hand on my arm and my heart speeds up. But his fingers just hover in the air for a moment, before he pulls his hand away.

I shouldn't let it bother me, especially with everything else that's going on. Cale made it clear how he felt about this Skin, and I get it. If he were the one using this Skin, I probably wouldn't want to touch him, either.

"I recorded last night's conversation." Finding the file on my band gives me something to look at other than Cale. When I start it playing, the Beast's head projects above my wrist.

Cale draws in his breath. "He looks exactly how I imagined."

The Beast glowers at me, and I switch the sound to broadcast so Cale can hear it. "It's only because we've known each other a long time that I'm giving you one last chance," the Beast snarls.

My voice plays, captured by the recording. "I haven't changed my mind."

The Beast's teeth grind together. He looks like he's only

hanging onto his temper with a mighty effort. "By working together, we've made our fortunes. We trusted each other. You know what I'm talking about."

I didn't know last night, and the mystery hasn't gotten any clearer since then. My voice plays again. "The increase isn't a big one. You can afford it."

"That's not the point, and you know it. You give those workers a single credit more, they'll think they can demand whatever they want." He shakes his head, his thick lips screwed up in a snarl. "If you won't listen to reason, you'll only have yourself to blame."

"What are you going to do?" The defiance I was feeling is clear in my voice.

His eyes narrow, almost vanishing into his fleshy face. "Seventeen years ago, you profited more than anybody else. But you won't always get to call the shots. Maybe you need to learn that the hard way."

"What exactly are you—?"

The recording finishes, and the Beast's head vanishes back into my band. He disconnected the call.

Cale's eyes are wide. "Seventeen years ago was the Welcon disaster. Is that what he was talking about? Did Morelle profit from it more than anyone else?"

I think back, trying to work out how big the Morelle Corporation might have been before the Welcon disaster. The Welcon anti-cancer vaccine caused a massive baby boom, and second-child taxes were introduced so New Triton could be built. I suppose people must have made fortunes along the way, but the idea of people profiting off so much misery turns my stomach.

"My father died paying second-child taxes," I say. "Welcon tore my family apart."

He taps his chin, his eyes unfocused and aimed toward

the ceiling. "I was only four when the Welcon disaster happened, but I'm pretty sure I've heard something about Edward Morelle expanding his factories. With the building boom, and a desperate workforce who'd work long hours for low wages, he must have had it made."

I clench my fists, fighting the urge to jump up and punch something. "If Morelle had anything to do with causing the disaster…"

"I don't think there's any way to know for sure. Besides, Edward Morelle is dead. He's not getting richer anymore." He twitches up one side of his mouth in a half-smile, and I can tell he's trying to make me feel better. "The new President Morelle is going to raise wages, no matter what the Beast threatens." Now he finally does put his hand on my arm, and the warmth of his touch drains my anger. "Just promise me you'll stay safe, Milla. He's a powerful man."

"What can he do to me when I'm more powerful than he is? He's only human, and this Skin is even stronger than my Leopard Skin."

"Does that Skin have the same effect on your human body?" His brow creases, worry in his eyes. "When you get hurt in it, does your human body get injured?"

"I don't know. Let's hope I don't find out."

He drops his hand from my arm and I instantly miss his touch. "Where is your human body?" he asks.

"In Edward Morelle's pod, hooked up to all the high-tech machines that kept him alive. Even if I get injured, those machines can heal any wound." I wave a hand dismissively, not wanting to picture my body in the coffin-like pod with all its hoses and tubes. "Anyway, the reason I asked you to come up here was so you could arrange a meeting for me. I want to talk to the Fist."

He blinks, frowning. "You what?"

"I know they won't want to see me. But I'm going to need their help."

His frown deepens. "I suppose I can set something up, but they'll be suspicious."

"I have food I want to distribute. New Triton food." I lean forward on the couch, pushing all my worries aside. "The wage increase will take a little time, but feeding my workers is something I can do *now*. Especially if the Fist agrees to help."

"You're going to hand out food at your shelters?"

I nod. "Better food than the workers are used to. It usually goes to some high-end stores in New Triton, but seeing as I own the factory that makes it, I can send it to the shelters instead." I study his face, hoping he likes my idea. After threats from the Beast, and worrying about both Ma and Tori, I really need something good to use up some of my energy on. "Ma and I used to pretend we were eating fancy dinners instead of the cheap sludge the dispensers spit out. Just for once, I want the workers not to have to pretend."

"Does Sentin know you're doing this?"

"I'm not going to tell him." When Cale raises his eyebrows at me, I meet his gaze with my chin raised. "He'll have a logical reason why I shouldn't, and I don't want to know what it is."

A slow smile breaks over his face. "Fair enough."

"You think I can convince the Fist to help? It's not the kind of food I can put in the dispensers. I need people to hand it out."

"I'll call Spade and Keren. They trust me, but even so, it won't be easy talking them into this. President Morelle isn't their favorite person." He grimaces. "In fact, they may only agree if they think it'll give them a chance to kill you."

My stomach tightens at the thought of my friends

turning on me, but I can hardly blame them. "I guess I'll have to take that chance."

SIX

"Ready?" asks Cale. We're in my private office on the one hundred and ninety-sixth floor of the Morelle Corporation building, standing in front of the opaque windows that let in light while hiding the view.

I drag in a breath. "Ready." Then I start the recording function on my band.

"This is President Morelle," I say in the New Triton accent that's starting to become second nature. "I publicly and officially acknowledge that the Fist is not a terrorist organization. Its members played no part in the bombings that started the Deiterran war. They've committed no crimes." Cale is holding up my speech, but I'm trying to sound natural and not like I'm reading it. "In fact, I hope to enlist the help of the Fist to make Old Triton safer. Therefore, I'm reaching out to key members, asking them to work with me to improve the lives of Old Tritoners. I want them to help me distribute food, medicine, clothing, and other necessities to Old Triton shelters." I pause for dramatic effect. "Up until now, I haven't had a good relationship with the Fist. The blame rests with me, and I sincerely hope they'll give me a chance to prove that we can make things better if we work together."

Cale gives me a thumbs up, and I cut off the recording.

"That was good," he says.

"You think the Fist will believe I'm being honest?"

He snorts out a laugh, as though I made a joke. "Not a chance. But it's a good start. I'll upload it to b-Net and Sub Zero, and send it to Spade and Keren personally."

"Thanks." While he does that, I settle behind my desk and pull up the records for my food manufacturing company. Math isn't something I'm good at, but if I ask Sentin for help, I'm pretty certain he'd try to stop me giving things away. So I'm the one who has to frown at pages of numbers, trying to work out the factory's daily production, and how much I can funnel back to the workers without going out of business.

By the time Cale interrupts me again, my brain aches, but I'm close to figuring it all out.

"Good news," he tells me. "Spade and Keren have agreed to talk. I'm amazed we've gotten this far with them already."

He taps his band's control panel to bring up his holo app, and two images are projected. Spade and Keren. I haven't seen them since the battle with the knights, and it takes all my self-control not to break into a grin.

They look pretty much the same, except Keren's arm is strapped up. That's right, she broke it in the battle. Spade's still wearing the same lumpy, knitted hat as last time I saw him, but it's even dirtier now. He's lean, and looks skinnier when he stands next to Keren. She's solid, with wide shoulders, and looks like she's wearing every piece of clothing she owns.

Keeping my expression neutral, I give them a polite nod. "Thank you for speaking with me."

"We saw your broadcast." Keren's eyes are narrowed, and she glares at me like she smells something bad.

"I want to distribute food to Old Tritoners," I say. "But I know what goes on in the shelters. The strong take from the weak. If we hand out anything, we'll need a way to make sure everyone gets their share, and help them keep it."

"How do you expect to do that?" Keren demands.

"The first step will be to get people to accept what I'm offering. They don't trust me, or the police force, or anyone who might be an obvious choice to help me. But they trust the Fist."

"Why would you suddenly want to give out food?" Spade snarls. "You've never done anything like it before." When he talks, I have to force myself to keep my gaze level and not stare at his mouth, at the dark spaces where his teeth are missing.

"Because I made a promise to Milla Scully," I say.

"What?" Keren's eyes go wide. "Where is she?"

"What have you done with her?" Spade hisses the question through gritted teeth and a muscle ticks in his jaw. As weird as this is, it's nice to see how concerned he is for me.

"She's busy doing me a favor." Impulsively, I add, "Actually, she's in Deiterra, with her friend Tori."

They exchange puzzled frowns, and I can tell I've shocked them.

Karen recovers first. "How do we know you haven't killed Milla? And Tori as well?"

"I'm sorry, I can't tell you any more than that." Mentioning Tori hadn't been part of the plan, and was probably a mistake. "They're both safe, and will be back soon," I add. When it comes to Tori, I sincerely hope that's true.

"So you're giving away free food in a shelter as some kind of payment to Milla?" Spade pushes his hat backward to scratch his greasy hair.

"That's right."

"How can we believe a word you say?" snaps Keren. "You executed four of our friends on stage in front of us."

"Things have changed. I'm no longer a danger to you."

"I'll vouch for her," Cale cuts in. "You can trust her."

Spade and Keren exchange more frowns, their doubt radiating off them. I can guess what they must be thinking. They're wondering what kind of pressure I've used on Cale to make him back me up, and whether I'm blackmailing or threating him. They're probably convinced this is some elaborate ruse to wipe out the Fist.

I drag in a breath and glance at the numbers I was going through, still visible on the desk holo. I hadn't intended to rush this plan quite so much, but if I'm ever going to convince them to help, I need to prove I'm serious. Besides, speeding things up is a good thing. I know what it's like to go to bed hungry. I used to get so desperate for anything to make my mind off my stomach, I'd chew my fingernails until they bled.

"I'm going to hand out food at one of my shelters tomorrow," I tell them, pretty certain I can make it happen. "If you come along, you can help me ensure everyone gets their fair share. But if the sharks operate unchecked..." I shrug. "Handing out food might do more harm than good."

Keren shakes her head. "As soon as we turn up, the police will arrest us."

"They won't. I'll come alone, with just a few guards. And with Cale."

"And a squad of knights waiting to burst in and take us

down?" Spade snorts. "You expect us to believe you're for real?"

"How about if I invite the media, and independent reporters can broadcast the whole event live to the feed?" I ask. "After the announcement I made today, trying to arrest you would make me look bad. It'd be terrible for my image, and there's an election coming up."

They don't look impressed, but it's all I can offer.

"I'll be there," says Cale. "And I can promise you, she's telling the truth."

"We'll think about it." Keren disconnects the call.

I turn to Cale, trying not to let him see that I already regret being so impulsive. Now I've committed myself to taking food to the shelter when there's a good chance the Fist won't turn up. Trying to distribute food without them is sure to lead to trouble.

Cale shoots me a smile. "Cheer up. That went better than I thought it would. You were convincing."

"Really? You think they'll actually turn up at the shelter?"

"I'll call them again later. Don't worry, I'll talk them into it." He nods at the holo display. "You understand all those numbers?"

"Weirdly, I've figured out what they mean." I lift a hand to flip through different spreadsheets. "This is a list of all the food we manufacture at the factory, with daily production totals. This one shows manufacturing costs, and here are the distribution details. I've been cross-referencing the numbers to work out what we can afford to give away." I screw my nose up. "Sentin was worried I'd bankrupt the Morelle Corporation. I'd hate to prove him right."

Cale blinks. "That's a lot to figure out."

"I didn't think I'd be able to do it, but it hasn't been as

hard as I expected." A flush of pride comes through in my voice. I've never done anything like it before.

Instead of looking impressed, Cale frowns. "The Skin must be affecting your brain. It's changing the way you think." The way he says it makes it obvious how much he hates the idea.

"Is it a bad thing if it makes me smarter?"

"How can you even ask that? What if it changes *every-thing*, and you lose who you are? What if you transfer back into your own body and you're not Milla anymore?"

"I'm still me."

He shakes his head, his jaw set. "It's not worth the risk. Give the Skin up. I'm pretty sure Sentin will agree to take over."

"Not until I've made Old Triton less of a hellhole."

"Is it worth letting your brain be changed by that thing?"

"Yes." I say it without hesitation, without even needing to think about it.

Cale stares at me a moment longer. Then he lets out a long breath. "I hope you're right," he mutters, turning toward the door.

I watch him leave with an uneasy feeling churning in my stomach. But as it turns out, organizing enough food to be delivered to the shelter so quickly keeps me busy enough that I don't have time to worry about anything else. I spend hours arranging it, and by the time I get to the shelter the next day, all I can do is hope that I haven't wasted my time. If Keren and Spade don't show up, the sharks will gorge themselves.

It's a weird feeling striding briskly through the doors of the shelter I used to live in, with my high heels clacking over the grimy floor. I left here with my wrists shackled, covered in Rayne's blood. Now I'm walking back in as the most powerful woman in Triton.

Life is strange.

Walking with me, alert for danger, are six of my personal guards. I could have brought a few of the forty-seven remaining knights instead, but they've killed too many sinkers for that to be a good idea.

Behind the guards, a couple of reporters are broadcasting my arrival, adding their own commentary so everyone in Triton can watch. The Beast might be watching as well. He might see this as an attack on him and the other industrialists. If I get my way, he'll be forced to start looking after his workers as well, so he'd better get used to it.

The shelter still stinks like old sweat and wet clothes. The smell is all too familiar, and if I close my eyes, the memory of my old fear is so vivid, I could almost go back to being the old me.

So I don't close my eyes.

Instead, I scan the large room, looking for Cale, who promised to bring Spade and Keren to meet me here.

I can't see Cale among the curious throng of people who're gaping at me. They've watched me on the holo plenty of times, and I remember how strange it was the first time I saw Morelle in the flesh. It feels just as odd to be on this side of the staring faces, especially when I recognize some of the workers who are gazing at me. Some are people I've worked with. One or two I'd call friends. And there are sharks, too.

I'm tempted to look for the shark who killed Rayne, and have to force myself not to. Anyway, what would I do if I found him? Arrest him for no apparent reason and have him hauled away? Sure he'd deserve it, but how would it look?

"There you are." Cale emerges from the crowd. With

his bronzed skin, tweaked face, and New Triton clothes, he stands out almost as much as I do. Unstained by the grey dirt that coats the floor of the shelter, standing in front of the crowd of thin, sunken-eyed workers, Cale looks like a movie star from the holo. It was how Rayne looked when she walked into the shelter wearing her beautiful blue coat. When I first saw Rayne, she made me feel like even more of a monster than usual. Judging by the way some of the sinkers are shrinking back as they stare at Cale, they feel the same way.

"Did Keren and Spade show up?" I hold my breath.

He angles his head toward my guards. "They're here. They'll come out if you lose your entourage."

"You did it." My chest lightens. "And they're not just here to kill me?"

He doesn't smile at my joke. "No guarantees," he says grimly.

I tell my guards to look after the food crates, which are being brought in and stacked in one corner of the large room, and Cale and I move to one of the dining tables near the food machines. Though that area is crowded, empty space immediately clears for Cale and me, so we don't have any trouble finding a vacant table.

When we sit down I lean forward and murmur quietly to Cale. "Everyone looks just as miserable as I remember."

He replies just as quietly. "Give it time. You haven't been President Morelle for long."

I'm not even sure why it's become so important to make things better for Old Triton. Maybe Cale's rubbed off on me. He's not even a sinker, and he's a member of the Fist, dedicated to helping a city he doesn't live in. Compared to him, I've been selfish. I only thought about my own survival for so long, I have a lot to make up for.

Keren emerges from the crowd with Spade behind her. Spade is limping, probably still feeling the effects of their battle with the knights. Keren treats me to a narrow-eyed glower, scratching her broken arm under its sling. Neither of them sit down, but stand on the other side of the table, keeping it between us.

"I don't blame you for being suspicious," I tell them. "In your place, I would be too. So thank you for coming."

"We brought plenty of friends," growls Spade. "If you try to arrest us, it'll get ugly."

I hook my thumb at the crates in the corner. "There's the food. I was honest with you. I really do need your help to distribute it."

Keren glances at the crates, then quickly back again, as though she's afraid my plan is to attack her while she's looking away.

"I'll need you when I bring in medicine as well," I add. "And other essentials, like clothing, and blankets for people to use on icy winter nights until I can I get decent heating installed." I stop, because how would President Morelle know how freezing it gets inside her shelters at night?

"Why are you doing this?" Spade scowls at me.

I stand up. "Help me hand out the food I brought with me, then we can talk."

Without waiting to see if they're going to follow, I cross to the stack of crates and direct my guards to start levering off the lids. Inside are boxes of food bars, the good quality ones, only sold in the best New Triton stores. They're called YumYum Bars, and they have a colorful wrapper, a sweet, melt-in-your-mouth flavour, and are packed with nutrients. According to the spreadsheets I went through, the Morelle Corporation usually sells them for about five times as much as they cost to make.

I brought enough bars for every grunt to have one. Tonight, at least, they'll go to bed with full stomachs.

When I turn, I find Cale right behind me, with Spade and Keren a little further back, gaping at the contents of the boxes. Behind them, the reporters are focusing their cameras on the stack of food, and probably zooming in for dramatic effect.

"How are we going to do this?" asks Cale, glancing behind him at the gathering crowd. "There must be, what, a few hundred people in here?"

"This shelter sleeps up to two thousand people. It has six levels." I turn to Spade and Keren. "You said you brought friends with you. We can hand out the food here, but we'll need help to make sure everyone gets to eat what we give them. You know how cut-throat this place is."

Keren blinks, her gaze still fixed on the food bars. "You have thousands of food bars?" She sounds awed.

"Two thousand."

"They must be worth a fortune." She tears her eyes away from the crates, looking around nervously and scratching her wide nose with the hand that's not strapped up. "A target for thieves."

"So? Want to hand them out? The reporters are watching, and this is your chance to show everyone that the Fist are the good guys." I eye the people who are inching closer. I doubt any will have been handed anything for free before, and they're bound to be just as suspicious as Keren and Spade.

A girl is standing to one side. Her arms are crossed and she's wearing a defiant expression that reminds me so much of Tori, my heart contracts.

I grab a bar out of the crate and toss it to her before she

can think about vanishing back into the crowd. She catches it by reflex, then blinks at it.

"Have you ever had one?" I ask. When she shakes her head, I motion for her to try it.

She rips the wrapper open and takes a bite. The crowd are all staring at her now, so they see the delight spread across her face as she chews. "It's good," she mumbles with her mouth full. "It's really good."

The reporters train their cameras on her, and I can't help but smile at her expression. I know all too well what kind of miserable day she must have had, slaving in one of the factories that now belong to me. Every day was the same when I lived here, and nothing good ever happened. If somebody had handed me one of these bars then, I'd have looked even more surprised than she does.

The people around her murmur to each other, then press closer to the crates, clearly wanting their own bars.

I tug a small tablet out of my pocket. Just like tossing the YumYum Bar to the girl, I throw the tablet to Spade. "Here's a list of everyone who sleeps in this shelter. They get one bar each, and they can swipe their bands as they collect their share. I'll have more food delivered tomorrow, so we need to get a better system going. We can do it this way once, but it's not going to work long term."

Spade stares down at the tablet. Keren keeps her gaze on me, with her eyes narrowed. Then her mouth firms and she gives me a nod. With her good hand, she grabs some bars out of the crate. "Listen up." The shout booms surprisingly loudly out of her short, wide frame. "You gotta line up to get your share, and swipe your band so we know you're done. One each, no exceptions. Move to the side to eat, and stay where we can see you. Then move on. Give us any trouble, or if we catch any thieving, we'll beat your sorry asses into the ground."

Cale shoots me a grin. "Looks like we're going to get it done." He grabs some bars and stands next to Keren as the crowd starts forming a line. "You'd better move back. Some people might not want to get in line if you stay too close."

I motion my guards to retreat with me, and we head toward the door. But I don't want to leave yet, in case Cale and the others run into trouble and need help. Besides, I want to watch people eat. Seeing their faces as they bite into the bars makes my chest fill with air, like I can lift off the floor and float away.

Leaning against the wall near the door, I watch as word about the food spreads, and people pour down from the shelter's other levels to join the ever-growing line. We're definitely going to need more Fist members to help with everything I have planned.

I want to make things better at every shelter, including the one Ma worked in. Maybe she'll even want to come and lend a hand. She must still have friends there, and she'll probably get a kick out of it.

Shame I can't distribute food in every shelter in Triton, but I doubt the Beast, or any other factory owner in his little club, will let me feed people in the ones they own.

A lot more people are eating now, and for the first time ever, the shelter is full of smiles. Tired faces have been transformed. A group of women are sharing a joke and laughing together as they wait for their turn at the front of the line. Such a simple thing to give out food, but the gift is lifting peoples' spirits.

This can't be a one-time thing. I need to make sure these people keep being fed.

What if I gave a food factory to the Fist? They could

run it, not for profit, but to feed Old Tritoners. And what if I—?

An alarm sounds from the door. A man is barging his way inside the shelter, and the scanners are flashing. The stompers who usually guard the doors are nowhere in sight, and the man's holding something shiny.

Heart thudding, I push myself away from the wall. The man has a popper. When he scans the room, his gaze falls on me and a slow, evil smile spreads over his face.

He's some distance away, and when he speaks I wouldn't be able to hear him if it weren't for my Skin's enhanced senses.

"The Beast sends his regards," he says. Then he draws his arm back and hurls the explosive at me.

SEVEN

As the popper arcs toward me, I grab two of my guards and yank them sideways, trying to drag them out of its path. In spite of the high heels and business suit I'm wearing, my Skin is fast enough to get away. But I can't leave the guards to get blown up. They're big men, slow and heavy, and their reflexes aren't nearly as sharp as mine.

The popper hits the wall where I was learning, and I pull the two men down to the ground with me, trying to cover them with my arms.

A heat wave slams into us, its force strong enough to tear me away from the guards and skid me further across the floor. The explosion is so loud, it sounds like the popper went off inside my skull. My skin feels like it's on fire.

I lie still, too shocked to move. Am I alight? The pain is lessening, and I don't feel so hot anymore. All I can hear is a loud ringing noise. I'm panting, but I can't hear the sound of my own breaths.

Hands touch me. Somebody grabbing me. I lift my head and stare into Cale's frantic expression. His lips are moving, but I can't hear what he's saying.

Behind him, something is on fire. Flames climb high, then cold water explodes from the ceiling as the shelter's sprinkler system goes off. The chill of the water is a welcome relief. I still feel crispy, but when I scramble to my feet and stare down at myself, I don't have so much as a scratch, let alone a burn. I may look human, but every part of this Skin is tougher than any person would be.

Sinkers push past us, running outside to escape the water that's raining down on us from the sprinklers. At my feet, one of the guards I tried to save is lying still, his skin burned. The other guard is a short distance away, and he looks almost as bad.

I start toward him, but Cale grabs my arm and shakes his head. "All your guards are dead," he mouths.

I still can't hear him over the ringing in my ears, but I nod. The stack of cartons with the food bars in them is on fire. The man must have thrown more than one popper, because there's nothing left of some of the crates but a mess of splintered wood and food chunks.

"Is anyone else hurt?" I ask Cale, barely hearing the words that come out of my mouth.

He nods, and points over to where Spade is crouched over, attending to some people sprawled on the floor.

"We need to get them some help." Water runs into my mouth when I talk, and the words buzz weirdly in my head.

"Already on the way." This time I hear him a little, though I still need to read his lips. "Come on." He leads me out of the shelter.

I look around for the man who did this, but he must be long gone. He did what he came for, and destroyed the one good thing the workers have experienced in who knows how long.

Anger rises in my gut.

The Beast doesn't get to ruin everything. I won't let him win.

As soon as we're outside, Cale turns to me. His gaze runs up and down my body, examining me, his expression worried. "You're okay, aren't you? You're not hurt and hiding it?"

"I'm fine." I run my hands over my arms, checking that it's true. The ringing in my ears is quietening, and I'm not in any pain.

"Okay." His frown softens. "You need to get out of here."

"But I need to make sure the injured are taken to hospital, and—"

"I'll take care of it. Having President Morelle here will just make things more complicated. Your guards are dead, and people might start to wonder why you're not, especially if anyone else decides to attack you, and you need to fight back. You won't be able to hide the fact you're so much stronger than a regular person."

He's right, but I hate to leave when people are hurt. Still, I let him lead me toward my car, which is waiting for me a short distance up the road.

The car door slides open, and he motions for me to get in. "Go. Please. I'll make sure everything gets cleaned up here."

"Wait. Are the reporters still here? Are they okay?" I scan the crowd of people who've already left the shelter.

"There's one of them." Cale points, and I spot a bedraggled-looking reporter leaning against the front wall of a neighboring building. Her face and clothes are filthy, but she's still holding her camera.

"Is my face as dirty as hers?" I ask Cale.

He gives me a puzzled look. "Apart from being wet, you look okay."

I run a hand over my dripping hair and check my sodden clothes, then cross to talk to the reporter. "I want to make a statement," I tell her, keeping my tone brisk.

She blinks at me, her expression dazed. "A statement?"

"That's right. Start recording."

She still looks confused, but lifts her camera and points it at me.

I clear my throat. My ears are still ringing, but I speak as clearly and firmly as I can. "A terrible act of terrorism has just occurred. As you can see, I was caught up in it, and it brings me great sadness to say that innocent people have been hurt or killed by a callous bomber." I motion to the milling crowd, and the reporter dutifully sweeps her camera around them before turning it back onto me.

A drop of water rolls down my forehead from my wet hair, and I blink it out of my eye. "As acting president and head of Triton's largest corporation, I have a responsibility to care for every citizen of Triton, including those who are living in my shelters and working in my factories. If this terrorist act has done anything, it's proven the need for urgent and immediate changes in *all* Old Triton factories and shelters. That's why I'm immediately putting in place new laws to improve security and safety. And all factory owners will need to provide better food and free medical care for those who need it." I stare into the camera, hoping my anger and resolve shows in my eyes, and that the Beast will see it. I hope this recording makes him spit with rage. He wanted a war? Now he's got one.

"The new laws will improve the lives of all Old Triton-ers," I go on. "It's about time factory owners looked after their workers and used their profits to make things better.

Starting now, every industrialist will take responsibility for the well-being of their employees. If they won't do it voluntarily, then I'll make them do it. That's a promise."

I can't think of anything else to say, so I motion for the reporter to cut off the recording. "You got that?" I ask.

She lowers her camera, staring at me with wide eyes. "I got it."

"Upload it to b-Net now."

She rushes to obey before I can change my mind. Her fingers are trembling, so hopefully the recording didn't wobble too much. I can hardly blame her. Only minutes after surviving an explosion, she's been handed an exclusive scoop with President Morelle that will probably make her career. No wonder she's a little shaky.

"It's done," she says, looking up. "Thank you, Madam President."

I nod, turning away. The recording should spread to Sub Zero quickly. In fact, I wouldn't be surprised if a 3-D image of my wet face is already appearing out of the bands of hundreds, maybe thousands, of people.

"Are you ready to go now?" Cale leads me back to the car. "That's if you've finished provoking The Beast?" He shakes his head, his expression rueful. "You never back down, do you?"

"I'm leaving, aren't I?" I look back at the milling crowd, still reluctant to just walk away. "You need to tell Keren and Spade that I'm sorry this happened, but I'm not going to let the Beast stop me."

"Don't worry about that now. Just take care of yourself."

All the way back to the Morelle scraper, I think about how I'm going to get payback for what just happened. By the time I get up to my private apartment, the ringing in my ears has gone, but my anger hasn't. All it takes is a little soap and water, and a change of clothes, and I'm ready to keep fighting back.

I've just finished getting changed when I hear the elevator. Sentin must be here, and I'm pretty sure he's going to be pissed off I didn't tell him about my plans to distribute food.

Sure enough, I find him in the living room, dressed, as always, in black. And yes, it suits him. But this time it seems symbolic, because I've put on a cream suit. It feels like we're like two opposing chess players lining up across the board.

I square my shoulders, ready for him to berate me, and already planning the arguments I'll use in my defence.

Frowning, he lifts one hand to grip my forearm. "Are you injured?" His gaze goes up and down my body in a way that reminds me so much of the way Cale looked at me that my heart does an unwelcome skip. Was he worried for me?

But no, that's silly. He's only worried that this Skin might have been damaged, not really about me. "No wounds," I say crisply.

He drops his hand. "Good."

"This Skin is fine," I add, crossing to the window. "No thanks to the Beast. He was trying to kill me, and didn't care who else he hurt."

"Do you understand the consequences if the President's Skin had been destroyed?" The tightness in Sentin's voice makes me turn back to face him. His eyes are darker than normal and his lips are pale. For the first time since I've known him, he's not entirely in control of his emotions. But is he angry? Or afraid?

"Blame the Beast," I say. "Not me."

"If President Morelle dies in public, we can't manufacture a new Skin and keep going. If that happens, everything changes."

I cross my arms. "There's only one way to make sure this Skin stays safe. Help me stop him."

Sentin takes off his high-tech glasses and studies the lenses as though looking for smudges. When he puts them back on, his emotions are tucked back out of sight. "I appreciate what you're trying to do." His tone is even. "But you're rushing through changes that Triton isn't yet ready for."

"Old Triton is more than ready for change."

"But New Triton isn't. And using that Skin means you can live forever. Stop trying to fix everything this week, or this month. Start planning for the next hundred years."

"Is that what you're doing?" I frown. "But you're not using a Skin. In your human body, you won't live forever. If you want to be around next century, don't you need to store your human body in one of those coffin pods that'll keep it pumped full of whatever chemicals Edward Morelle was dosed with?"

"A pod is the opposite of a coffin. Think of it as a time capsule. When your body is inside it, you're outside of time."

"You didn't answer my question. Are you going to use one? And are you planning to take this Skin away from me?" I lift my chin. "Because I won't let you have it. Not if you don't care about Old Triton."

"I'm not about to take that Skin from you."

I narrow my eyes at him. "Why not?"

"If I used a Skin now, I'd lose the Deiterrans' trust. We need to negotiate a peace treaty. That's my priority."

"And after the negotiations?"

He quirks an eyebrow. "Do you *want* to keep that Skin?"

"I do." It's not until the words are out of my mouth that I realize how important the president's power has become to me. Helping Old Triton has given me a sense of purpose that's bigger than anything I've felt before. Maybe I'd be willing to give the Skin up if Sentin felt the same way, but if he doesn't care about Old Triton, he could be as bad—or worse—than Edward Morelle was. He might decide to leave Old Triton the way it is, so New Tritoners can stay rich and comfortable. I'm not willing to take that risk.

I draw in a breath, a rush of resolve heating my blood. "You can't have this Skin. And another thing. I'm not going to Deiterra with you until I've dealt with the Beast."

I expect Sentin to get angry, or demand that I go. Instead, he turns and motions for me to follow. "Come with me. I want to show you something." He walks toward the stairs that lead to the garden at the very top of the building. A robot gardener is tending the plants, and the room is humid, with the ventilation system emitting a steady hum. Up here, the air is thick with the scent of damp earth and growing things. All the walls and ceiling are uninterrupted glass, and the view takes my breath away.

"What do you see?" Sentin nods toward the windows.

I frown, confused by the question. "Skyscrapers. Triton and Deiterra. And a lot of sky. Why, what do you see?"

He turns to the glass, and his gaze grows distant. "I see a blueprint. I don't limit my vision to what exists today. Instead, I picture what could be there in the coming decades. Looking over the entire city, small problems become insignificant." He turns back to me, his eyes catching mine. "If you let go of your petty concerns, we can remodel Triton and Deiterra into a single utopia. You and I could do it together."

An unwelcome warmth spreads through my chest. I've never had someone ask me to change the world with him before. I've got to admit, it's a powerful offer. But for some reason, I feel like I'm betraying Cale by even considering it.

"*Petty* concerns?" To cover my uncertainty, I sound more offended than I really am.

He inclines his head. "The workers in Old Triton aren't starving. Their existing food rations provide sufficient calories for their daily needs."

I huff out a breath. "Shows what you know."

"You're focusing on trivial things. Instead of concerning yourself with minutiae, start thinking on a much larger scale."

"Trivial? You wouldn't think it was so trivial if you were the one going hungry." I shake my head. "How can you make everything wonderful unless you fix what's already broken?"

"You're not an Old Tritoner anymore, Milla. Come up from the darkness and look at everything that's laid out in front of you. There's more on offer than you realize." He sounds like he's talking about the view, but then he steps closer to me, his eyes searching my face, and with a shock, I wonder if he's talking about himself, telling me to look at *him* differently.

But that's a crazy thought. Sentin couldn't be suggesting I see him in a romantic way.

He's taller than I am, so I have to tilt my head back to look into his face. He's bathed in the light that's pouring through the windows, and he's wearing a snug black T-shirt and black jeans that emphasise his lean build. His scent is as complicated as he is, both sweet and spicy, like licorice and aniseed.

"We need to go to Deiterra," he says. "The meeting's arranged, and this is our chance to negotiate peace on our terms." Instead of his usual matter-of-fact tone, there's a hint of a question in his voice. As though he's asking me to understand how important this is to him.

"But I can't let the Beast get away with what he did today." I shake my head, wrenching my gaze from his.

Sentin sighs. "The Beast can wait."

"You don't understand how vulnerable the people of Old Triton are. They have no protection against people like him." I nod at the spectacular view. "Those scrapers go on forever, and they're all full of people. No wonder New Tritoners forget there's a whole other city underneath them. And all the way up here, it'd be even easier to forget. But I can't do that."

"You can't see the bigger picture." It's a statement rather than a question, and it's tinged with disappointment. Was Sentin hoping I'd choose his grand plan and stop caring about Old Triton?

"I'm only where I am because of dumb luck," I tell him. "If Rayne hadn't walked into the shelter that night, I'd still be there. If I were still alive, that is, which is doubtful, seeing as Tori had just been sent away. I probably would have been shark bait, dead in the dirt. She died instead, and I got lucky."

He tilts his head, his voice going unexpectedly soft. "That Skin is changing you in subtle ways, and I thought it might make you narcissistic, but the opposite is true. You fought to get where you are, yet you're not giving yourself enough credit for what you've achieved."

My face warms and I glance away to hide my surprise. Sentin's never like this. He's distant and unemotional. He doesn't give out compliments that make my heart beat faster.

"Now I want to fight for all the people who didn't get

lucky," I say. "Maybe I feel guilty because I made it out and they didn't. Whatever. I can help them, so I will."

"A war with the Beast isn't productive. Besides, he's far more ruthless than you are, and he's demonstrated a willingness to endanger the people you're trying to protect. Strategically speaking, it would be difficult for you to win a fight against him."

"But when it comes to strategy, I have a secret weapon."

"What's that?"

I shoot him a hopeful look. "You."

EIGHT

"The soldiers are all here," Sentin tells me in a low voice. "All but the forty-seven who'll remain as knights."

I nod, though Sentin's wrong about one thing. Morelle's young, brainwashed soldiers aren't all here. William is missing, because I sent him home with Ma.

We're standing in the lobby of the Meat Locker. The last time I was here, I used a Knight Skin to get in, and wiped the chips of hundreds of soldiers before carrying William out. This time, the soldiers are lined up in rows, standing to attention in the giant room that used to hold over a thousand pods. I can still see the marks the pods left on the concrete floor. Without them, the place is an endless, echoing chasm that still reeks of sweat.

The soldiers are mostly teenagers, with a few older ones here and there. There are just over one thousand of them, all standing stiffly in an identical position with one hand to their forehead in a held salute.

I watched some of them use their Knight Skins to kill innocent people, but I have to keep reminding myself that it's not their fault. The reason they're killers is because Edward Morelle made them that way.

"At ease," I say, sending my voice through my band so it projects through the enormous room.

All of their hands snap down at the same time. They stare straight ahead, their eyes lifted to the space just above my head, awaiting my orders.

I'm about to break their hearts.

"The Knight Skins are gone," I say in a firm tone. "Permanently. The ones you used have been destroyed, and I'm not making any more of them."

I pause to let the soldiers react. Most give me a shocked, wide-eyed stare, before managing to drag their gaze back to the wall above me. Some go pale. A few sway. They don't make any sounds, let alone protest or break ranks, but they have to be feeling the same way I did when I lost my Leopard Skin. Like they're never going to be fully alive again.

I take a breath, and keep my voice hard. "From now on, your job will be to make Old Triton safe. You'll patrol my factories and shelters, and guard the vulnerable. You'll take care of the weak, and make sure there are no more attacks, bombings, rapes, or murders in Old Triton."

It's a dangerous move, turning these young soldiers into a new form of stompers. The Knight Skins made them ruthless, and Old Tritoners have no defence against them if they decide to keep up their reign of terror. But the soldiers have been idle since the Fist destroyed most of the Knight Skins, and hopefully by giving them a sense of purpose I can help them change for the better.

"I have rivals who are trying to hurt me," I announce. "You've all heard about the attack on the shelter yesterday. I need you to keep watch and make sure nothing like that ever happens again."

I sweep my gaze around their faces. Either their shock is fading, or discovering they're going to be guarding against a real threat has perked them up. There's a new lift to their chins, and a hardness in their eyes that I hope is determination.

"Do you understand your new role, soldiers?"

"Yes, Madam President." The shout comes from every mouth, in perfect unison. It's so loud, the walls vibrate.

"You'll be closely monitored. If I hear of anyone stepping out of line, there'll be no second chances. Any soldier who even thinks about hurting one of the people you're supposed to be protecting will be discharged." I pause to run a stern gaze along the lines of Old Triton faces. "Is that clear?"

"Yes, Madam President." The shout is loud enough to hurt my ears.

I nod at them, turn, and walk out. I've already briefed their commanding officers, and Cale has asked the Fist to keep a close eye on them.

Still, I'd feel a lot better about this if I hadn't agreed to leave for Deiterra tomorrow, and was here to monitor them myself. Instead I'll have to trust their officers to obey the strict rules I've set.

"That was a good start," I tell Sentin in the car as we head back to New Triton. "But it's the next part that I'm looking forward to."

He frowns. "This is more risky than I'd like. I'd prefer if you didn't go through with it."

"Oh, I'm going through with it. And thanks for arranging it, even though you're against it."

"If I didn't, you'd do something even riskier."

I shoot him a grin. "You know me too well."

Our car locks into the bullet track, lifting out of the darkness of Old Triton and into the brightness of the city above. I lean forward, peering out of the window at the skyscrapers coming into view. The one I'm searching for is tall enough to stand out from the buildings around it, though it's still dwarfed by the Morelle Corporation building.

"That's the Beast's scraper?" I ask, pointing.

Sentin nods. "Phoenix Industries." He checks his band. "The knights are arriving now."

I rub my hands together. "This is going to be fun."

Sentin heaves an exaggerated sigh, taking off his glasses to pinch the bridge of his nose.

I laugh. "Come on, can you really tell me you're not going to enjoy this? The Beast had his shark throw poppers around a crowded shelter. He deserves worse than a little scare. In fact, he's lucky I'm not planning to march into his office with some explosives of my own."

He shakes his head, his expression serious. "We agreed that you'd deliver your warning, and leave without incident. I expect you to keep your side of the deal. Remember, nothing is more important than our trip to Deiterra."

When the car pulls up outside the front doors of Phoenix Industries, I find forty-seven knights waiting for me, as promised. They're lined up on the sidewalk, standing to attention. Their huge bodies look threatening even when they're just standing still, especially because their over-sized arms hang to mid-thigh. They're killing machines, pure and simple.

"Stay here," I tell Sentin, sliding out of the car. But he's already getting out of the other side.

When he strides up to the knights, they salute, then

stand to attention. "This is a non-violent mission," he announces. "Your objective is to intimidate, but you may not injure civilians or destroy property. Is that clear?"

"Yes, sir." The response booms from forty-seven obedient knights.

"Thanks, Dad," I mutter to him. Then I raise my voice. "Ready, knights? Follow me."

I march into the scraper with the knights on my heels. The loud stomping of their metallic boots on the ground no longer gives me chills. Hopefully today, the sound will scare some New Tritoners for a change.

On the other side of the building's big, marble lobby is a reception desk with a startled-looking woman standing behind it. But I already know where I'm going, and lead the knights to the elevators behind her.

"Excuse me." Her voice shakes as she calls after me. "May I help you, Madam President? I'm so sorry, but will you allow me to announce you before you go up?"

I turn and give her a pleasant smile. "Certainly. Please tell the Beast we're coming for him. Let him know that if he's not already in his boardroom on the top floor, he'd better hustle his ass up there before we start breaking things."

There are far too many of us to get in one elevator, so I keep pressing the button until eight elevators have arrived at ground level. We all get into them at once, and arrive on the top floor of the building at the same time. I stride out first, and all the knights spill out after me, organising themselves into orderly rows.

There's a small waiting area outside the elevators, and large double glass doors that lead into the Beast's enormous boardroom. Instead of pushing the doors open, I ram my fists into them with all my strength, one into each door. It hurts the hell out of my knuckles, but they shatter into a million tiny pieces with a very satisfying sound. When I step forward, my heels crunch the glass into the Beast's plush carpet.

Inside the boardroom, six men are sitting at the large table. The Beast pries his huge bulk out of his chair at the head of the table, nodding as though he was expecting me. The receptionist must have warned him we were on our way.

"President Morelle. Welcome." His big lips twist up into a smile. "I believe you know everyone here."

The five other men at the table all stand too, and I realize I do know them. At least, I recognize their faces from the holo. They're all wealthy, and they own factories. They look enough alike that they could be brothers, but I guess that's just the tweaking. Maybe they all used the same surgeon. With his bald head and fleshy face, the Beast is the only one who stands out.

"I assembled our consortium so we could all speak together," says the Beast. "Won't you sit down and join us?" He motions to the knights who are standing stiffly behind me, ready for anything. "Your soldiers are welcome to wait outside."

My glee is disappearing fast. I expected to surprise him, and it's disconcerting that he's acting like I've arrived late to a meeting he invited me to attend. My plan was to barge in so I could threaten him with violence if he hurt any more people. But now that he's invited me to join them, I might as well hear what they have to say.

Leaving the knights where they are, I ease myself into one of the seats at the table. "So, talk."

The Beast and the other men all sit too, and I feel a moment of total unreality. It wasn't so long ago that I spent my days punching out pieces of metal in a factory, and now I'm seated at an opulent boardroom table with the most powerful men in Triton. The view from the full-length windows isn't nearly as good as the one from the Morelle scraper, and of course we're not tall enough to see over the Deiterran wall, but it's still impressive. And this room is even more richly decorated than Edward Morelle's boardroom. The table looks like it's been carved out of gold, there are rich red flowers everywhere, and a large bronze sculpture of the Beast's ugly face is displayed against one wall.

The Beast smiles at me again, his fleshy cheeks squashing into balls. "As you know, we're reasonable men." He motions to the others at the table. "If you stop being foolish, we can all be friends again."

One of the other men speaks up. "If you insist on giving free meals to workers, I want compensation for all the food I won't be able to sell them."

Another man slaps his palm on the table, a scowl twisting his chiselled lips. "I don't see why you had to break our deal in the first place. You build an army, and you think that entitles you to bankrupt us?"

"Now, now, gentlemen. No need for raised voices." The Beast turns to me. "Withdraw your attempt to raise the minimum wage, and we may be willing to discuss some alternative proposals for the other suggestions you've made."

"I'm not withdrawing anything."

The Beast clicks his tongue in disapproval, then leans forward to pick up a round glass ornament that's decorating the table. Settling back in his chair, he tosses the ornament casually from hand to hand. It has a small red flower encased inside it, and looks heavy. Like a solid glass baseball.

"Let's cut to the chase," he says. "Either we come to a deal that suits us all, or you'll regret it. That's a promise, and I'm a man of my word."

I put both hands on the table, watching him closely so I can snatch the ornament out of the air if he throws it at me. "I'm raising the minimum wage, giving away food and medical supplies, and doing everything else I promised. If you don't like it, that's too bad."

The men mutter angrily to each other, but only the Beast speaks up.

"If you won't negotiate, then your fight is with all of us," he says. "Not just with me."

"As you say, I have an army." My voice is cold. "Why should I negotiate?"

"To avoid any further unpleasant incidents like the one you experienced at your shelter." The Beast is still tossing the glass ball from hand to hand, and it reminds me of the popper his would-be assassin threw at me. "I'm sure you want to avoid killing any more innocent people?" He raises his eyebrows, smirking like he's said something funny.

"If you so much as think about killing any more people, I'll have you arrested and charged with murder."

The Beast chuckles. "I don't believe there's a judge in Triton who'd allow me to spend even a minute behind bars."

"Then I'll let the knights deal with you."

"You're welcome to try, but it's already been established that your Knight Skins have vulnerabilities. And you're aware that Harrison here manufactures the weapons used by our brave police force." He nods toward one of the men at the table. "We're far from defenceless."

Harrison speaks up. "When you think about it, we don't

even need to destroy the knights. We only need to get to you. And there are six of us."

The man opposite him leans back in his chair, looking smug. "You may be the richest of us, but when we combine our resources, we have far more than you do."

"And I know your darkest secrets." The Beast tilts his head. "For example, I know you can't be Edward Morelle. You must have stolen his Skin. So who are you?"

My stomach swoops. None of the men at the table have reacted to his announcement, so it's not a surprise to them.

"I don't care what you know, or what you have," I snarl. "Threaten me or anyone else, and you'll find out how strong my knights really are."

The Beast catches the glass ball in one hand, then slowly stands up. His huge bulk takes up almost as much space as the knights do, and when I get to my feet, I feel tiny in comparison.

He lets out an exaggerated sigh. "If you refuse to see reason, I'll be forced to ask you to leave so we can continue our meeting without you. Allow me to escort you to the elevator." With the glass ball clutched in one hand, he walks around the table toward me.

My first instinct is to take a step back, but I've been around enough sharks not to show anything that could be mistaken for fear. "I'll leave when I'm ready," I snap.

He stops next to me. "You've said what you came to say, and now we all know where we stand. Unless you're going to order your knights to kill us here and now, we have nothing more to talk about."

I hesitate, tempted to command the knights to attack. But Sentin already ordered them not to hurt anyone or damage any property. What if they obey him and not me?

"This was just a warning." I turn and stalk back toward

the elevators, motioning the knights to follow. "Next time, my soldiers won't leave so easily."

The Beast follows me through the smashed door to the elevators. Then he stops and leans close. "It doesn't matter who you are or how you obtained that Skin. If you go on this way, we'll take you down."

I draw myself up, adrenaline coursing through my veins, making my blood pump hot. "How do you think you'll do that? Maybe you know this is a Skin, but you clearly don't know how strong I am, or you wouldn't dare threaten me."

His face flushes. "You think you're stronger than me?" Lifting the hand that's holding the glass ball, he squeezes. The solid ball shatters into a thousand slivers of glass.

I gape at his hand as he crunches what's left of the ball, letting the pieces fall through his fingers. The glass didn't cut him. He doesn't have so much as a scratch. And no human could possibly be that strong.

The Beast lets the glass fragments drop away, until all he's holding is the small red flower that was in the center of the ball. He shakes it to ensure it's free from glass, then hands it to me with a sarcastic bow. His fingers are twice the size of mine.

NINE

"Did you know the Beast is using a Skin?" I demand.

Sentin blinks slowly. "Contrary to what you seem to believe, I can't know everything."

I exchange a glance with Cale. We're in my car, heading toward the breach in the Deiterran wall. Cale seems excited to see Deiterra, and Sentin's been pushing hard to make this trip happen. I'm the only one who's reluctant to go.

"How many humanoid Skins do you think there are?" asks Cale.

Sentin shakes his head. "I have no idea, though I've always assumed Edward Morelle made more humanoid Skins than just his own. The technology is an immensely valuable commodity, so it makes sense that Edward would exploit it." He looks up, his eyes going distant, as though he's making calculations in his head. "Of course, the Beast is wealthy enough to fund his own scientific research and development teams. If Edward sold him a Skin, he's almost certainly used it as the basis for his own work. He could even be at the point of being able to manufacture his own Skins by now, though Edward would have been foolish not to have retained an exclusive license for commercial distribution."

We're close to where the hole was blown through the Deiterran wall, and the closer we get, the more I want to stop the car and take the knights back to Phoenix Industries.

I blow out a frustrated breath. "Leaving now is terrible timing. We need to go back and find out what the Beast is up to. We can't let him think he can do whatever he wants."

Cale frowns. "What if the other men you met in his boardroom were using Skins? If the confrontation had gotten physical, it would have been six against one."

Sentin's jaw tightens. "In that respect, the consortium of industrialists aren't the only ones we need to worry about." He brings up his band's controls and selects a recording. A hologram projects above his band. It's a Knight Skin. As the camera pulls back, I see the Skin is inside a small, white room, surrounded by other machines. Wires snake out of it, and numbers cascade down the screens it's hooked up to.

"This footage was recorded in a laboratory in Deiterra," Sentin says. "They have a number of Knight Skins there, presumably collected after the Fist launched their attack on the Meat Locker and disabled some of the Knights that were engaged in combat on the other side of the wall." From the look he gives us, I guess he knows it was me and Cale who wiped the soldiers' chips.

The holo image zooms in, focusing on the Skin's head. I'd thought the knights' armor was unbreakable, but its head has been cracked open like an egg, and its brain matter scraped away to expose the circuits embedded in the tissue.

"What are they doing?" I ask.

"The Deiterrans are reverse engineering the Skin technology. They're developing their own Skins."

Cale frowns. "Creating their own Skin army?"

Sentin nods. "The knights came close to penetrating the palace and ending the imperator's rule. He'd be foolish not to want to use the same technology as a means to fight back."

"In that case, we need to stop them." I let out a long breath. "But if they're putting together their own Skins, what makes you think they'll want to negotiate a peace treaty?"

"I don't believe they have everything they need to be able to activate the Skins. But the longer we delay our trip, the longer they'll have to perfect the technology."

The car stops. Fallen buildings block our path so we can't drive any further. From here, we'll have to walk.

"What exactly are we going to say to the imperator?" I ask.

"The Deiterran imperator is a difficult man. He keeps the country under tight control, and our negotiations will require delicacy."

I expect Sentin to say more, but instead he opens the car door and gets out.

Cale meets my gaze. "That wasn't an answer," he mutters.

I grimace, and go after Sentin. For the first time since transferring into the President's Skin, I'm wearing comfortable clothes. Not quite as comfortable as the jeans and T-shirts Doctor Gregory gave me when I first arrived at the Morelle Corporation, but at least my shoes are flat-soled and practical. The trousers and blouse I have on are formal enough not to feel under-dressed if I'm wearing them when I meet the Deiterran imperator, but I should be able to walk a long distance in them. And the knights are carrying our luggage, in case we need to stay in Deiterra for a night or two.

The ground here is uneven, littered with rubble though we're still a reasonable distance from the breach. I pick my way through the debris with Cale by my side. Behind us, all the knights are marching together. Their boots crash to the ground in unison, in spite of the rocks strewn over the ground.

They're all coming to Deiterra with us, to protect us in case the imperator decides it's easier to kill us than strike a peace treaty. I'm trying not to be alarmed by the fact Sentin thought we should take all forty-seven knights with us. But I guess it's better than leaving them behind.

I call ahead to Sentin. "Aren't you going to tell us more about what we're getting into?"

He stops and waits for Cale and me to draw level with him. "What do you want to know?"

"Everything. Anything." I motion for the soldiers to stop marching. "How about you start by telling us why you've always refused to say anything about Deiterra."

"Because that information is classified."

"Classified by who?"

Sentin gives one of his slow blinks, and I think it's his way of expressing shock that I'd ask a question with such an obvious answer. "Triton is severely overcrowded. What would happen if fifty million people learned how much space there was on the other side of the wall?"

"The Fist would find a way to blow up the wall," says Cale.

"Anarchy." Sentin nods. "The information was suppressed for fear of sparking an open revolt. If I were to speak openly about Deiterra, I would have been arrested."

A horrible thought occurs to me. I move close to Sentin and drop my voice to a lower murmur, trying to make sure none of the knights can hear us with their bat-like ears.

"Does the imperator know it was Morelle who blew the hole in the wall? I mean, does he think I did it?"

Sentin shakes his head. "Fortunately, the imperator is certain that President Trask ordered the wall destroyed." He speaks in the same low tone, bending so his lips are near my ear. "The imperator is aware of how vulnerable he's become in recent years, and assumes the President considered him an easy target."

Cale is bent close too, the three of us in a private huddle. Cale's cologne mingles with Sentin's, and both scents fill my lungs. Cale's is fresh and crisp, while Sentin's is a rich spice with a tantalizing hint of sweetness.

My senses are so sharp, I can also detect both the wound on Sentin's palm where he cut himself on the broken glass from Felicity's window, and the faint tang of the healing spray he's coated it with.

"Why is the imperator vulnerable?" asks Cale.

"When the wall was built, Deiterra was a progressive society. Since then, Triton has continued to advance while Deiterra's technology has stagnated. When the knights invaded, Deiterra could offer little resistance."

I glance back at the knights, picturing them sweeping through Deiterra, slaughtering everyone they saw. It's easy enough to imagine after I watched them mow down the Deiterran fighters who tried to attack through the breach in the wall.

"Why hasn't Deiterra kept up with our technology?" I ask, supressing a shiver.

"It's a rural economy with a comparatively low population base. Rather than having democratic elections, the Deiterrans are ruled by a single autocratic family. That family has always believed in preserving the integrity of their agricultural lifestyle. Schooling is considered to have been completed after the student graduates from a secondary level, and the imperator hasn't prioritized innovation."

"When was the last time you were in Deiterra?" I ask curiously.

His eyes focus on me. The bright sunlight turns his irises more silver than gray, reminding me of his Reptile Skin. "I left when I was fourteen."

"Do you miss it?"

A cloud passes across his expression. "No." He glances down, and I get the impression he's remembering something unpleasant. Then he gives his head a small shake, as though dismissing whatever happened to him in Deiterra. "We should keep moving. The imperator is expecting us."

He motions to the knights and starts walking, obviously done with answering questions.

"Before going through the wall, I'd like to know more about what's on the other side," mutters Cale.

I nod. Sentin told us more than he normally does, but I'm still itching to turn him upside down and shake all the secrets out of his brain. There must be deep hurts in his past, but they're buried deep and he's obviously reluctant to go digging for them.

I guess I can relate. Butterflies and rainbows weren't a feature of my childhood either.

Cale and I follow Sentin, and when we get close to the breach in the wall, he stops again to let us catch up. The knights stop behind us, somehow managing to stand in formation, though we're surrounded by enormous piles of concrete and steel debris.

This is where Tori went through the wall.

Thanks to the mountains of rubble, it's difficult to tell how wide the opening is. Part of New Triton collapsed, so there are actual apartment buildings lying across the breach. The wall's a lot taller than Old Triton, perhaps as much as one hundred stories tall, and rubble descends from the damaged section like giant stone waterfalls. It's as much a labyrinth as an opening.

At least we don't have to worry about the wall's automatic defence system any more. If Triton still had aircraft, we probably could have flown to the other side without being shot down.

"So we just walk through?" asks Cale. "And the Deiterrans will be waiting for us on the other side?"

"That's right."

Cale glances at me. "Tori went through at night. Maybe the Deiterrans didn't see her. She might be taking a good look around Deiterra."

Sentin shakes his head. "Your friend shouldn't have tried to get in. She'll be a prisoner by now, if they haven't already executed her."

My stomach drops. "You have spies over there, right? Somebody must have given you that footage of the Knight Skins. Have you heard anything about Tori?"

"I haven't received any word about her, but I know the imperator."

"If he's hurt Tori—"

"Even if he has, the peace we're going to negotiate is too important to jeopardise." Sentin fixes me with his direct gaze, his jaw set. "If the Deiterrans develop their own Skin army and launch a counter attack, millions could die on both sides of the wall. Is that what you want?"

"Of course not." Irritated, I press my lips together. Tori's my best friend. How am I supposed to shrug it off if the imperator's hurt her?

"Don't you think you should tell us more about the

imperator?" Cale sounds as worried as I am. "Milla needs to negotiate with him. She should know his strengths and weaknesses."

Sentin shakes his head. "I'll be the one negotiating the deal. President Morelle is merely accompanying me to give legitimacy to our agreement. The imperator won't speak with her directly."

"He sounds like a great guy." Cale blows out a loud breath. "So we can't do anything to help Tori, and have to wait around helplessly while you do all the talking?"

"I'll let you know if I need you to do any more than that. Now, shall we go?" Without waiting for an answer, Sentin starts forward, picking his way through the debris.

Following him, I catch a glimpse of green. It's the giant tree I spotted last time I was in front of the wall. The sight makes my anger slip away. In spite of my fear for Tori and unease about meeting the imperator, my heart starts beating faster. I'm going to walk through the green fields of Deiterra. The thought fills me with awe.

But first we need to pick our way across the broken concrete and rock, passing the remains of peoples' shattered lives and destroyed homes. I see filthy rags that may have once been clothes, broken electronics, and even a child's pink sandal. I can only hope its owner is still alive.

Then the wall itself is looming on either side of us, and our path turns into a trail that's been cleared of rubble.

The closer we get to the tree, the more enormous it seems to get, until it's towering over us. And as we emerge from the shadow of the wall, the sun hits us. Though we're on ground level, like Old Triton, it's as hot and bright as New Triton. Not for long, though. In front of us, shade is cast by the tree's enormous branches. And there's not just one tree. There are hundreds of them. From my window in the Morelle scraper, the trees look a lot smaller and almost insignificant compared to the expense of green behind them. From here, the giant trees are jaw-dropping.

"What kind of trees are they?" I ask Sentin, my voice coming out breathless.

"Different kinds. They mostly bear hybrid fruits, bred to withstand the heat." He points to a cluster of smaller trees with bare trunks and huge leaves. "The only non-hybrids are those banana trees."

"Banana trees," repeats Cale. "You mean, like the fruit?"

"The food that's marketed as bananas in Triton doesn't bear much resemblance to the fruit that grows on this tree."

Whatever food they're talking about must only be available in New Triton, because I've never heard of it. "Will we get to taste it?" I ask.

Sentin's lips quirk up in one of his rare smiles that transform his face. When he smiles like that, it's easy to forget how secretive he can be.

"There's a popular fairy tale in Deiterra about a child who ate so much goldenfruit, he turned yellow and grew roots of his own." He points to some heavy golden pods hanging beneath the leaves of one of the trees. "You'll no doubt try a variety of Deiterran fruit, and after you do, you may not want to leave."

Cale shades his eyes, peering toward a different cluster of trees. "I see soldiers."

Sentin looks too. "They're called legionnaires."

A structure has been built into the trees. It's a long, squat building, covered with branches and foliage. It's well camouflaged, but with my sharp eyesight, I should have spotted it right away.

Sure   enough,   several   soldiers—legionnaires—are

marching from the building. A few are olive skinned, but none look like they've been tweaked. Their faces have the same uneven features as sinkers, and one man has a scar pulling up his top lip. They're wearing khaki uniforms, and carrying large rifles.

"Stand down," I order the knights behind us, just in case any get it into their heads to do something foolish. We stop and wait for the legionnaires to approach. They're not pointing their rifles at us, but they're not putting them away, either. They're holding them in two hands, ready to fire if they need to.

I stand stiffly, unwilling to make any move that might be misinterpreted. I've always hated guns.

They march up to us and stop in front of Sentin, ignoring Cale and me altogether. They're not wearing bands, and it's jarring to see them walking around openly with naked wrists. Of course we're not subject to Triton laws over here, but it still makes me feel uneasy.

The legionnaire in front salutes Sentin. "We're here to escort you to Reliance, sir."

I exchange a wide-eyed glance with Cale. Why did the soldier call him *sir*?

Sentin nods at him. "Lead on, tribune."

The legionnaire doesn't move. "I need to ask if your companions have any weapons, sir. We've been ordered to confiscate any we find."

"Only the knights have weapons. The rest of us have none."

"My orders are that the knights may come up to the outskirts of Reliance, but they can't come inside."

"Very well. Your terms are accepted."

The legionnaire salutes again, then the entire troop all

pivot at the same time and march away. Sentin walks behind them without looking back.

Cale and I frown at each other, and I can tell he's wondering the same thing I am. How does Sentin expect the knights to protect us if we're leaving them behind?

TEN

This part of Deiterra has no roads, only dirt paths that look like they've been worn into the ground over many years. Around us are the green fields I'd imagined walking through, and the reality of them is even more incredible than I dreamed.

I'd pictured grass, because of the small parks they have in New Triton. But the plants in these fields are nothing like grass. The ones nearest us are tall, with large flat leaves, and they're planted in neat rows. The plants in another patch are even taller, with long, thin leaves. And there are short plants with tendrils. The fields seem to go on forever, with only a handful of people working amongst all the greenery.

In Triton there are crowds everywhere you look. A population of millions, and barely space to breathe. I've spent my life working and sleeping in buildings crammed with people, so to see this huge expanse of land with hardly anyone in it feels dizzying. My gut keeps trying to tell me something must be wrong, as though the entire population has fled from an unknown disaster.

Cale and I are walking together, with Sentin and the Deiterran legionnaires a small distance in front, and the knights marching behind us. The few people in the nearby fields stare at us, their expressions hostile. One old man spits on the ground, then makes a gesture that I have no problem in recognising as obscene, though I've never seen it before.

"They don't like us," I say, stating the obvious.

"Do you blame them?" asks Cale. "Our knights came to their side of the wall to fight their legionnaires."

I glance over my shoulder at the Skins marching behind us. The sunlight glints off their black armor, and their heavy footsteps are throwing up a low cloud of dust. "It's a shame we had to bring them. They couldn't look more menacing if they tried."

Cale's mouth twists. "I'm more worried about what's going to happen when we're forced to leave them behind."

Once we're well past the people who were staring at us, I look back to see them returning to their work, bending down to the soil. Harvesting their plants? Caring for them? I know nothing about growing food.

"I wonder if they use robots here," I say, thinking of the gardener who looks after Felicity's garden.

Cale shakes his head. "I think they must be tending to the plants by hand. If they had robots, surely we'd see them."

"What kind of plants do you think they are?"

"Different types of food, I suppose."

The plants don't look anything like any food I've ever seen, and it's hard to imagine wanting to eat something that's been lying in the dirt.

"I think I'd prefer a YumYum Bar," I murmur.

Cale brings up his band's control panel, then frowns at

it. "I wanted to see if there's any information on plants, but I can't connect to the feed."

"What?" I tap on my own control panel. "I'm getting error messages too."

"We must be out of range of the Triton network."

"So we won't hear about anything that happens while we're gone?"

"I guess not."

I should be used to being without a band, but maybe it's because I had to go without one for so long that not being able to connect makes me so uneasy. The worst part will be not knowing what's happening in Triton. The Beast could be attacking my factories, or the ex-knights I sent into the shelters could be wreaking havoc, and there isn't a thing I'll be able to do about it.

"Look!" Cale points.

I follow his finger to something big behind a large patch of very tall plants. It's a huge brown animal, even bigger than my Leopard Skin, with four legs and a long head. I've seen animals like that on the holo, but I never thought I'd get to see one in real life.

"Is that a horse?" Cale breathes the question, and I'm too shocked by the sight to do more than nod.

We stare at it wordlessly. It's in a pen on a large square of ground that's almost bare, stretching its neck over the wooden fence, reaching for plants to eat. Its tail flicks from side to side as it chews.

For quite a distance beyond its pen, the ground is black instead of green. It looks like a fire may have burned through here, destroying all the plants. And in the middle of the burned ground is the charred remains of a structure.

A woman walks out from behind the tall plants, near the horse. She spots us and freezes, staring wide-eyed from beneath her wide-brimmed hat. She looks terrified, and I have an overwhelming urge to call out, so I can reassure her we're not here to hurt anyone. Before I can, she ducks back into the tall plants.

"They're all wearing big hats and long sleeves," says Cale. "And none are wearing bands. Have you noticed?"

"The big hats must be to protect them from the sun. I wish Sentin had suggested we bring some of our own. The sun's getting fierce." I wipe the sweat from my face. At least this Skin has been tweaked so I won't get as sunburned as I did in my human body.

"Did you expect it to be like this?" he asks.

"How could anyone have expected this? It's like we've gone back in time. Way back."

"Into a holo movie," he agrees. "One with cowboys."

"Is all of Deiterra like this?" I wonder aloud. "Or just this part?"

"You should catch up to Sentin and ask him. He's more likely to answer your questions than mine."

"Why do you think that? He barely tells me anything."

Cale shoots me a sideways look. "The only time I've ever seen a smile on his face is when he's looking at you."

I frown, trying to think whether that could be true.

"Good thing I'm not the jealous type," he adds, his lips quirking up to tell me he's joking.

"Jealous?" I shake my head. "How can you be jealous when you can barely stand to get close to me anymore?" In the whirlwind of becoming President Morelle and trying to change things for Old Triton, I've missed the easy way we used to be with each other. I hate that there's a distance between us now. He used to touch my arm when he spoke, or take my hand. Now every touch is grudging.

He gives a one-shouldered shrug. "When you're in your real body, I'll gladly go back to the way we were."

I press my lips together, not wanting to say what I'm thinking. What happens if I never stop using this Skin? I can do a lot of good for Triton in it, especially if I win the presidency. According to Sentin, I could live forever in it.

"Look." Cale points at a branch that's jutting out above our heads. He's probably just trying to change the subject, but when I glance up, I see small red fruit hanging enticingly down, a little out of reach.

I stop, staring upward. If I jumped, I could grab one. But I can jump higher than a regular person, and the knights behind us might wonder why I'm so athletic.

One of the knights walks forward while I'm hesitating. "Please allow me, Madam President." He has the voice of a young man, my brother's age or a little older. He reaches up with one oversized arm to pluck a fruit, then offers it to me.

"Thank you." I lift the fruit to my nose to inhale its scent. It's like nothing I've ever smelled before.

"Begging your pardon, ma'am." The knight inclines his head, and his tone becomes apologetic. "It was presumptuous of me to come forward and offer help before being asked, but that's the way I was raised."

"What's your name?"

"It's Clayton, Madam President."

"You're an Old Tritoner?" I already know he is. His accent is pure Old Triton.

"Not anymore, ma'am. I'm just a knight."

I fight the urge to sigh. It's not his fault that Edward Morelle brainwashed him. "What about the mother who raised you so well, and taught you such polite manners? Are you looking forward to seeing her again when we get back?"

"My mother died, ma'am. And I like being a knight."

He sounds a little uncertain now, like my questions are some kind of test.

"Were you one of the soldiers who fought in Deiterra?" I ask.

"Aye, ma'am."

"How long were you here?"

"Three days, ma'am. We tangled with some Deiterran legionnaires just over there." He nods to the burned section of ground, with the charred structure in the middle. "We wiped them out and kept advancing. Another squadron took us on over there." He points into the distance, and I squint into the sun and make out more burned ground.

"You killed a lot of legionnaires?"

"Aye, ma'am."

"How do you feel about that?" I gaze up at his helmet, wishing it were possible for his black, armored face to show his emotions.

He's silent for a moment, and I can imagine his confusion over my questions. It's not really fair of me to punish his kind act with an interrogation.

"Did we do something wrong, ma'am?"

"No, Clayton. I'm the one who did something wrong." I glance at Cale. "I don't think the Deiterran imperator will want to make peace with someone who ordered the killing of his legionnaires."

"I'm sorry, ma'am." Poor Clayton sounds stricken.

"Don't be sorry. It's not your fault." I give him a nod. "Thank you for the fruit."

He salutes and goes back to his place behind us, joining the rest of the knights.

"Sounds like they left a trail of destruction," says Cale.

I nod, bringing the fruit back to my nose to inhale its scent again.

"You'd better check with Sentin before you taste that." Cale motions at the fruit. "Make sure it's not toxic."

"I'll talk to him now." I quicken my pace to catch up with him, and Cale lets me go ahead. As I approach Sentin, I can't help but feel self-conscious. Is it true he only smiles at me? And if so, what does it mean?

The dirt path is only wide enough for two people to walk abreast, and the Deiterran legionnaires are marching in pairs, leading our party and trusting us to follow. Sentin is walking directly behind the last pair as though he's one of them.

Is he a legionnaire? Or a spy? Maybe he's been living in Triton all these years so he can watch us and report what we're doing to the imperator.

"Hey." I draw level with him, then slow to match my pace to his. "Is it safe to taste this?" I hold up the piece of fruit. What I really want to ask him is why the legionnaire called him sir earlier, but coming right out with the question would probably guarantee he doesn't answer it.

He nods. "It's a type of plum, genetically engineered for year-round fruiting. Residual toxins from the soil will be in its flesh, but ingesting one fruit won't cause any ill effects."

"So that's a yes?" I take a bite. The taste explodes in my mouth, first a little bitter, then it becomes sweet. The red skin is almost like a membrane stretched over a mushy center. It's so juicy that red liquid runs down my chin. "Delicious," I mumble, wiping my chin with my free hand.

Sentin's lips twitch, like he's trying not to laugh. "The juice will stain your clothes."

I jut my head forward to stop it dripping on my blouse, and take another bite. "There's something hard inside," I mumble with my mouth full.

"That's the seed. It's inedible. Eat around it, then you can drop it."

I do what he says, then lick my fingers clean. "I can hardly believe I ate something that grew on a plant, something with a *seed*, which, let's face it, sounds pretty disgusting. But it tasted amazing."

"You think food manufactured from chemical compounds is more palatable?"

"Not any more."

My response is so enthusiastic that his lips hitch up again. "There'll be many different foods to try here. Try not to give yourself a stomach ache."

Can this Skin get stomach aches? As far as I can tell, I've been fuelling it pretty well just by eating normally. Surely it has the same nano-technology that keeps New Tritoners from getting sick?

"Not all of these plants are for food." Sentin reaches out and plucks something small and brown off one of the plants. "See this nut? Once the hard outer shell is crushed, the liquid inside is bright yellow. It's used for manufacturing dye."

"Crush it so I can see?"

"The shell's too hard to crush by hand. The process is done with machinery."

"I bet one of the knights can crush it." I look back at the knights and call, "Clayton."

The knight who picked the fruit for me strides past Cale to catch up with me. "Aye, Madam President?"

"Would you please crush this?"

Obediently, Clayton squeezes the nut. When he opens his black hand, it's covered with a yellow fluid, so bright it's iridescent. He lowers his face to peer at it. "What's this goo?" His tone is fascinated. Then he remembers who he's speaking to and his head snaps up. "Sorry, Madam President."

"It's a nut that makes dye," I tell him. "Thanks for demonstrating."

He gives me a sharp salute, the yellow stain already drying on his hand. When he goes back to his squad, Sentin and I resume walking.

"Is it strange for you to be back in Deiterra?" I ask Sentin. "Has it changed?"

"So far, it's just the same." Sentin answers with no emotion in his voice, so I can't tell if he thinks that's a good thing or not. But something tells me this isn't a line of questioning that's likely to get him talking.

"They don't have any roads here?" I try instead.

"This is a rural area. There are cities with roads, though compared to Triton, they're more like small towns."

"Is Reliance a city?"

He nods. "Reliance is the largest city in Deiterra. It's where the imperator will host us in his palace."

Just ahead are several large, round structures, giant metal balls suspended off the ground. Behind them is some complex-looking machinery, and there are several pipes snaking from them that run along the ground and disappear into the fields. At the base of one metal ball, liquid is dripping, forming a large, muddy puddle.

"What are those?" I point to them.

"Water storage. They pump water from beneath the ground, to irrigate the land."

"They get water from the dirt? Do people drink it?" I grimace, thinking of the filthy water that collects in puddles on Old Triton streets when it rains. The water supply in Triton comes from desalination plants on the coast.

"It's purified to remove residual toxins from the food wars. I think it tastes better than Triton's water."

I'm about to express my disbelief, when I spot something. Half hidden among the plants, several fat birds are pecking at the ground. I point them out to Sentin. "What are they?"

He cocks his head, lifting one eyebrow. "You don't recognise chickens?"

I'm not even sure why I'm so surprised that there are chickens walking around. After all, I've just seen a horse. But before the Welcon disaster, there were still one or two chicken factories in Triton, and my parents used to talk about how they'd save up to buy real eggs. I've always thought that was strange, because the documentaries I've seen have stressed how inhumane it was to keep animals locked in tiny cages, and how much better off we are now that our food is manufactured.

"How come the chickens are running around free?" I ask.

"Because this isn't a poultry farm. They probably belong to the farmer."

Rather than answering my question, that just confuses me more. But there are lots of other things I want to know, and if I ask him to explain, Sentin's likely to waste time telling me about the intricacies of chicken farming.

"Everything's so different from Triton," I say. "Do you still have family living here?"

"My grandparents live in Reliance. If they're still alive, that is."

"You don't know if they're alive?" It's strange that he managed to get information about the Deiterrans developing Skins, and not about his own family. "But you'll get to check in on them while you're here?"

He shakes his head, and I have to clamp my jaw down on the burning urge to ask why not. If he doesn't get on with them, it's probably a subject he doesn't want to talk about.

"And your mother?" I ask instead.

"She's in Triton." He hesitates a moment, then shoots me a sideways glance. "She's never been to Deiterra."

I gape at him. "You lived here without her for ten *years*? From the age of four to fourteen?"

"My father wasn't supposed to marry a Tritoner, let alone have a child born on the wrong side of the wall. The imperator ruled that I'd be banned from Deiterra forever, unless my father sent me here for a minimum of ten years, to be raised as Deiterran by my grandparents."

I let out a low whistle. "That's tough, being sent away from both your parents."

"If they hadn't sent me to be raised here, I wouldn't have been able to negotiate this peace treaty." Though he's making light of it, he's walking with his shoulders slightly hunched, and there's a tension in his body as though he's remembering a bad time in his life. Sentin's emotions are always buried deep and hard to sense, but I get the feeling his time in Deiterra might have been difficult.

"Not much comfort to a four-year-old boy," I say sympathetically. He and his father must have had a complicated relationship. I can't imagine my father ever agreeing to send me away at such a young age.

Sentin doesn't answer. He looks like he's too busy concentrating on the placement of each footstep, even though the ground's even, and walking is easy.

"May I ask you a question?" I ask after a while.

He brings his gaze up to flash me a tiny glimpse of his smile. "It's a little late to ask for permission, isn't it?"

"I don't think you'll want to answer this question, and I

don't want you to go silent, or change the subject. I *need* an answer."

"Now I'm curious." He raises his eyebrows, silently inviting me to continue.

"Who are you loyal to?" I ask. "Deiterra or Triton?"

"Why should I be loyal to a place?"

Now it's my turn to be silent, because I don't know how to reply. It never occurred to me he wouldn't be.

"In Deiterra, they call me a Tritoner. In Triton, a Deiterran. They're both right and they're both wrong. Why should I be either?"

I think of the way Brugan taunted him, and the Deiterran who made the obscene gesture. "Then why are you here?" I ask. "Why is this peace treaty so important to you?"

"Because I'm shaping the future I want to live in."

"What exactly does that future look like?" Waiting for his answer, I catch my lip in my teeth. If he'd only tell me the truth, I'll know whether we want the same things and if I can trust him.

We round a bend in the path, coming out from behind some tall plants, and he nods ahead. "There's Reliance."

"That's Reliance?" I shade my eyes against the sun. Though he's distracted me from my question, I'm determined to ask it again as many times as I need to, until he gives me an answer.

In the distance is a low cluster of buildings, much smaller than I expected. The city almost disappears into the surrounding countryside, and some of the structures in front are just black frames. "Have those buildings been burned?" I ask.

"They were grain silos. The knights torched them to destroy the Deiterran's food reserves."

"Why?"

"To force the imperator to surrender with the least amount of bloodshed." His brow furrows as though he's disappointed I've asked such a basic question. "Winters here are as cruel as in Triton. Without the food stores they've built up, many will be at risk of going hungry."

"Burning their food is pretty ruthless, don't you think?" I don't know why it disturbs me more than the thought of flat-out murdering people. Killing soldiers is bad enough, but deliberately starving the Deiterran population seems evil.

"It was my idea."

I open my mouth and close it again, not sure what to say. But he can probably read my expression pretty clearly, because he adds, "If they'd surrendered, Deiterra would have become a protectorate of Triton. I would have ensured we increased capacity at our factories, and exported sufficient supplies to feed the population over winter."

"Oh." I should have known he'd think of everything.

"The grain shortage is an incentive for them to negotiate the peace treaty. They'll ask us to pay reparations for the damage done by our knights."

"What else will they ask for?'

"That remains to be seen."

"And what will *you* ask for?"

One of the Deiterran soldiers appears in front of us, and salutes Sentin. "Sir, the cars are just ahead. We'll take you to Reliance, then transport your knights to the barracks we've provided for them, just outside the city."

He leads us on a little further. Sure enough, a road cuts through this field, its black surface dusty. Some odd-looking machines are stopped on one side of it. Though there's no traffic, the cars have been pulled over so far to the side, their tyres are in the dirt. They're nothing like the driverless pods we have in Triton, with their circular shape and glass tops. These cars are at least double that size. Their shape is long and rectangular, and they have no tops, but are open to the air. In the front is a mechanism that I assume is used for manual steering.

We stop to stare at them, and Cale moves next to Sentin, touching his arm to get his attention. "If the knights are staying somewhere else, how will they protect us?"

Sentin blinks. "We'll remain in communication with them," he says in an 'of course' tone.

I shake my head. "Our bands don't work here. We already tried."

"We must be out of the Triton communication zone," adds Cale.

"The knights have inbuilt transmitters to create their own encrypted swarm network. I've patched into it, and I can do the same for both of you. I'll just need to change your band's settings."

I bring up my control panel so Sentin can connect me to the knights' network, then he does the same for Cale. When he strides off to address the knights, I exchange a look with Cale that tells me he's thinking the same thing I am. Sentin has all the answers, but he's giving us small servings of information as grudgingly as food gets dished out in a shelter.

While the knight that's carrying our luggage puts it into the car, Sentin orders them to stay in the barracks until we collect them. "But if we call on you, come immediately to the city." He points to the buildings in the distance. "Once there, you know how to protect us."

It sounds like a threat, and I can't help staring at the Deiterran legionnaires to see if they're going to react. But they don't look surprised or upset by Sentin's order. I guess it's what they were expecting. Maybe he even said it for their benefit.

The knights all stay standing at attention while we get into one of the cars with some of the legionnaires. In this landscape, the Knight Skins look even larger, blacker and shinier than they usually do. They're completely out of place here, and I can only hope they won't get into any trouble.

We settle ourselves in the car, and when it starts up, it surprises me by emitting a loud hum. The cars in Triton are silent, but the noise this one makes sounds like the whir of the conveyor belt in the factory I used to work in. I wonder what's powering it?

Sentin is sitting next to me. He bends his lanky body a little, moving his mouth close to my ear. My heart leaps. Has he decided to answer my question about the future he's trying to create?

He speaks so quietly that even with my enhanced hearing I can barely hear him.

"When we meet the imperator, you must say nothing."

I frown, pulling away so I can shoot him a questioning look. "Why?" I mouth.

"You're not Deiterran."

Great. If there weren't soldiers with us, I'd say something about how stupid that is. But I guess I'll need to put up with being a silent bystander while Sentin makes all the decisions.

I sigh and stare at the squat buildings in front of us. One thing I can say about this car, it's fast. The city of Reliance is quickly getting closer. Hopefully there, the million questions I still have might be answered.

ELEVEN

So this is Reliance.

The biggest city in Deiterra, but can it really be called a city when there are no scrapers at all? None of the buildings are more than two or three stories tall. Most are made of some kind of natural stone. I can't see any built with steel or concrete, which are what all the buildings in Triton are made of.

As our car winds its way to the imperator's palace, Cale and I stare at the narrow streets, fascinated by this view of lives so different to ours. A few people are walking along sidewalks, probably headed to jobs or whatever schools they have here. Their hair and clothing styles aren't unlike the ones on our side of the wall, but so far I haven't seen anyone with an obviously tweaked face.

With the car open to the outside air, the wind that blows over my face smells surprisingly clean, even fresher than the air in New Triton, and nothing at all like the constant pungent tang of urine, sweat, and filth of Old Triton. The streets are quieter here than on the other side of the wall. There are no street stalls, and no rough sleepers. The houses are built separately without sharing any walls, and some even have gardens between them, as though they have all the space in the world.

With the legionnaires watching, I don't want to seem like I'm gaping open-mouthed at everything. But it seems so far from the bustle and crush of Triton, I can't imagine what it must be like to live here.

Eventually, we pull into a driveway that cuts through an expanse of grass so green it doesn't look real. The mansion we stop in front of is enormous. Not tall, but wide and sprawling, far wider than any building I've seen in Triton. It's white, with ornately-carved columns around its girth, and large, elegant windows.

This has to be the imperator's palace.

We pile out of the cars, and a couple of the legionnaires bring our luggage. The legionnaires march us inside, showing us into a lobby with marble floors, and walls that look like wood and are a deep, rich brown. They could even be made of real trees.

A woman in a stiff white dress greets us, takes us down a long hallway, and ushers us each into a separate bedroom.

"Please rest," she says. "His Excellency has invited you to dine with him. I'll collect you at six o'clock."

She closes my door firmly, as though she expects me to stay inside. The bedroom is as extravagant as everything else in this place, with a large bed, some enormous closets, and an attached private bathroom.

I wait a minute or two until she's likely to have left, then open my bedroom door and peer into the hallway. The door of the next room opens, and Cale pokes his head out.

"Come in here." He motions me into his room, which turns out to be identical to mine.

"Can you believe this place?" I ask, sitting down on his bed. It's covered with a silky red cloth that feels cool and luxurious under my hands.

He closes the door. "I'm glad I came with you, to see it for myself."

"Crazy as it sounds, the entire way here, I kept looking for a glimpse of Tori. As though she might happen to be walking along the street."

"If she's still wearing her band, she might have location tracking on." He pulls up his own band's control panel. "The swarm network Sentin set us up with seems to be working. I'm getting no signal from Tori at the moment, but if she finds a network and manages to connect to it, I should get pinged. It's a long shot, though. It doesn't look like the Deiterrans have their own public network."

"Thank you." I let out my breath, trying not to get my hopes up. "And maybe our hosts will show us more of Deiterra. We could ask for a tour and use the time to search for her."

"I'd like to see more of Deiterra anyway."

"Me too." Getting off the bed, I go to the window to gaze out at the wide expanse of green grass outside. Even if we were here forever, I don't think I'd get tired of looking at it.

"Did you see this?" Cale opens one of the large closets, and it's not actually a closet at all. Inside is a mini kitchen, with a bench top and sink. Instead of a food production unit, there's a round metal canister full of water, and a bowl of real fruit. Now the closet door's open, the fruit's scent is strong enough to make my head swim.

I pick up a round, yellow fruit that's about twice the size of the one I ate on the way here. When I hold it to my nose, its fragrance is better than perfume.

"It smells like orange juice." I say.

"Maybe it's an orange."

I bite into its skin, but it's thick and bitter. Now though, the smell is even stronger, and a little moisture leaks out from inside. When I pull off some of the outer skin, the juice that runs over my hands is delicious.

Passing the fruit to Cale, I lick my fingers. "Did you ever think you'd get to taste a real orange?"

He puts some of the inner flesh in his mouth, then closes his eyes and groans. "I've never had anything like it."

I grab another piece of fruit from the bowl. "I want to try all of it."

"Me, too. Instead of having dinner with the imperator, I'd rather stay here and gorge myself."

My stomach turns over at the reminder of the important meeting about to happen. I don't know why Sentin seems so certain we can negotiate peace. We attacked Deiterra, then blamed the war on them. They have good reason to hate us.

"Are you nervous?" Cale asks.

I blow out a loud breath. "Why would I be nervous? We're in a foreign land, we have no idea who we're dealing with, and they might easily decide to kill us instead of negotiating with us."

He shoots me a sideways look, and I realise that of the three of us, I'm the only one who won't actually die if they do kill us. I didn't understand Sentin's quantum entanglement explanation, but as long as he's right about the consciousness transfer back to my human body working over such a long distance, I'll just wake up back in Triton, in Edward Morelle's pod.

"Sorry." I grimace. "I'm sure Sentin wouldn't have agreed to this meeting if he thought they'd execute us."

"He does seem to know everything before it happens." Cale scrapes the last of the orange's flesh off its thick skin with his teeth, then leaves the peel on the counter and washes his hands in the sink. "I'm starting to wonder if we're just actors who don't realize we're playing parts in a movie Sentin's directing."

"It does feel that way," I agree.

"Want to go and get some rest before the meeting?" he asks.

I shake my head. Give up alone time with Cale? No way. "Let's talk first, then I'll go and wash up." I sit back on the bed, curling my legs up on its silky cloth. "What do you think it'd be like to live in Deiterra? And where do you think all the people are?"

He sits down too. Not close enough that we're in any danger of touching, but not so far as to make me lose hope of him ever getting used to this Skin.

"They didn't have the Welcon disaster on this side of the wall," he says, leaning back on his hands.

"But even before Welcon, Triton was overcrowded. Why do we have so many people when they have so few?"

"We don't know anything about their lives. Maybe they're not allowed to have children."

I shake my head. "That can't be it. On the way here, I saw a couple of kids walking down the road."

"Then it's a mystery. We'll need to draw up a list of things to ask Sentin about." He shoots me a smile that flashes a hint of dimple. "Sentin loves answering questions, so I'm sure he'll be eager to tell us everything."

I smile back. After all that's happened, just to know that I can still sit and talk like this with Cale is a relief. When we joke together, the weight of responsibility eases from my shoulders a little. Or maybe it's just easier to bear. Without him, I'd be so busy thinking about what to say to the imperator, I'd have tied myself in knots by now.

"You're right." I keep my voice as light as his. "Sentin talks too much. I wish I could get him to stop with all the explanations."

Cale's expression turns serious. "Speaking of explanations, what was with the legionnaires calling him sir?"

"That should definitely go on the list of things to ask him."

Cale gets up to take another piece of fruit from the bowl. "Do you think everyone here eats food that's been grown on trees? I mean, all the time?"

"Judging by all the gardens, they must."

"Imagine living in all this space." He holds the fruit to his nose, but doesn't bite into it. "Now we've seen it, would you want to move here? Hypothetically speaking, I mean."

I shrug. "It seems like paradise, especially compared to Old Triton. But this place must have its drawbacks too. We just don't know what they are yet."

"I'd like to grow something and eat it."

"How long do you think it takes to grow food? Say, that piece of fruit?" I nod at the mottled yellow-green globe he's holding to his nose.

"Weeks or months, maybe? A lot longer than pressing a button to make food come out of a machine."

He offers the fruit to me, and I take the first bite before passing it back. We eat and talk about everything we've seen so far until it's time to get ready. I go back to my own room to wash and change into clean clothes, and just before six o'clock, the woman who showed us to our rooms reappears. She leads the three of us down several long hallways, to a luxurious sitting room with gold and white walls. It reminds me of a movie I once saw that was set in the eighteen hundreds. There are chairs grouped together that we could sit on, but Sentin stays standing, so Cale and I do too.

A waiter offers us drinks, and I accept a glass of something cold and delicious, that gets warmer as it goes down my throat. I take a bigger gulp and Sentin shoots me a warning look.

"The drinks are alcoholic," he murmurs. "Sip it slowly. Try to copy everything I do." Leaning in close to speak to me, his cologne fills my senses with the sweet and spicy scents of licorice and aniseed.

Sentin puts his untasted drink down on a small coffee table. I take one more sip of mine, then reluctantly do the same. Though it tastes nothing like street brew, I'm willing to be cautious. Cale keeps hold of his glass, as though he's decided the taste is worth the risk of getting drunk.

A young man comes into the dining room. He's wearing a silky white shirt and black trousers, and looks to be in his mid-twenties, barely older than Cale or Sentin. He has olive skin, but it's light enough that I doubt he's had melatonin added. He has an attractive face, but his nose would be considered too big in New Triton, and his dark eyebrows are crooked and overly bushy. In fact, everything about him looks natural, as though he hasn't been tweaked at all.

Sentin dips his head in a respectful semi-bow. "Prince Otho, we're honored to meet you."

I'm glad I put my drink down or I might have choked on it. A prince who looks like a sinker? They can't have tweaking over here at all.

The young man extends his hand. When Sentin takes it, he bows over it rather than shaking it. Then he glances at us, clearly wanting us to do the same.

"This is President Morelle, and Cale Rickard."

I take his hand and bow like Sentin did, and Cale does the same.

"A pleasure." The prince sweeps us with a wide smile that looks genuine. "My father will be here soon, but I'm glad we get a few minutes alone. I want to hear all about Triton."

Sentin nods. "Certainly, sir. What would you like to know?"

Prince Otho waves his hand in an exaggerated gesture. "Everything. No, wait. Tell me about the Skins first, then everything else. And there's no need to be formal with me. You can call me Otho." He looks at Cale. "You were in the Skin Hunter contest too, weren't you, Mr. Rickard?"

"Please, call me Cale. I wasn't in the contest itself, but I used the Saber-Toothed Tiger Skin for a few weeks."

"What was it like using the Skin?"

Cale glances at me, and I sense his hesitation. He's wondering if Prince Otho is looking for information to help his father's efforts to reverse engineer the Skin technology. It sounds like the prince is a genuine fan of the contest, but his boyish enthusiasm could be just an act.

"The Skins combine animal and human DNA," says Sentin. "Autonomic bodily functions are controlled by the Skin's brain stem and central nervous system."

The prince nods politely, but the spark in his eyes dims just a little.

"Their biological tissue is grown around a synthetic core," Sentin continues. "The transferral technique—"

"They were a lot of fun," Cale interrupts. "Can you imagine racing up a tower in a body that's several times stronger and faster than your own? It was the most exhilarating thing I've ever done."

The prince grins, the sparkle coming back to his eyes. "I'd give anything to be able to try it."

"Perhaps you could visit Triton and use one of the Skins from the contest." Cale flicks a questioning glance to Sentin.

Sentin nods. "Of course."

"But I've heard you lie in some kind of pod to transfer out of your body. Is that necessary? I'm not comfortable in small spaces."

"You suffer from claustrophobia?" The spark of interest in Sentin's tone is subtle, and if I hadn't gotten to know him over the last few days, I probably wouldn't have caught it. But for some reason, Sentin's gaze has sharpened on the prince.

Otho chuckles uncomfortably, his cheeks reddening like he wishes he hadn't mentioned it. "When I was a boy, I managed to get myself trapped in a tiny storage closet. Pitch black in there and hellishly uncomfortable. It was several hours before anyone found me. A little longer, and it wouldn't be such a funny story. The air was getting thin."

"You don't need a pod," Cale assures him. "The ones we used checked our vital signs, and kept our human bodies hydrated and our muscles stimulated. But all that isn't necessary if you only use the Skin for a few hours."

"In that case, I'd like to experience what it's like to use a Skin." The prince leans forward, talking only to Cale now. The two of them seem to have forged an instant connection. "Which of the Skins—?"

The sound of the door opening interrupts him, and we all turn to look at the uniformed staff member who's bustling noisily in, clearing his throat. "Presenting his Royal Excellency, the Imperator of Deiterra," he announces.

A man strides in behind him, wearing long golden robes, so long they sweep the floor. Their opulence is made even more impressive by the imperator's height. He's taller than both Sentin and Cale, and much taller than I am. He's bald and barrel-chested, but his face isn't nearly as fleshy as the Beast's. His features are craggy instead and his nose is bigger and more hooked than his son's. If he were a Skin, I'd be sure he had some eagle DNA mixed in.

"Your Excellency." Sentin bows low, holding himself down for a second or two at the bottom of his bow.

Cale and I glance at each other, then do the same.

"Welcome." The imperator's tone is dismissive, as though we're not welcome at all. "Formal negotiations will take place over dinner. Until then, I wish to hear about the assassinations of President Trask and Vice President Burns. And our esteemed ambassador, whom I'm told fell victim to an explosion."

"Of course, Your Excellency." Sentin bows again, just his head this time. "We have had a certain amount of civil unrest. However, democratic elections will be held in a few months, and until then, President Morelle is acting President of Triton."

The imperator turns his gaze onto me. His eyes are brown, but nothing like Cale's. The imperator's are as dark as some of the patches of soil I saw on the way here, where seeds must have been freshly planted, and the ground was wet.

"I've come here because I want peace between Triton and Deiterra," I say.

Sentin frowns at me. Too late, I remember he told me not to say anything. But what does he expect me to do, stand around like an ornament?

"Negotiations will take place over dinner." The imperator looks down his beaky nose and speaks in a clipped tone, as though telling off a child. "Until then, we will discuss the current situation in Triton."

I press my lips together and suck in a long, silent breath. This is already promising to be a very long evening.

"Your company developed the Skins," the prince says to me, his smile gone. "You created the army that attacked us. How can we believe you want peace now, when you're the one who—?"

"That's enough." The imperator cuts him off with a glare.

There's a noise from the door, and I turn to see two men and a woman entering. All three are wearing army uniforms, with medals pinned to their chests.

A staff member introduces them, and I immediately forget their names. All three are legates, which I guess must be the top rank in the legion.

They all accept one of the strong drinks from the waiter, then stand ramrod straight with serious expressions, as though it's a toss-up whether they're planning to salute or sip their drinks.

"President Morelle." One of the legates addresses me. "Please tell us, how many Skins do you have left?"

Sentin turns his calm gaze on the man and speaks for me. "I'm afraid that's classified. We brought forty-seven with us. That's all the president is prepared to say."

"The Skins did a lot of damage here. They wiped out several food stores. Then, all at once, they simply collapsed." The legate's eyes narrow. "Why?"

"The soldiers' chips were wiped," says Sentin.

"Yes, we know," the imperator cuts in. He makes an impatient motion with the hand holding his drink, causing the liquid to slosh in the glass. "But why? Who did it?"

"I believe I mentioned our civil unrest. There was a

short-lived rebellion against the authority of the president, but the insurgents have now been dealt with. The president is once again in full control."

I keep my expression blank, but can't stop myself from meeting Cale's gaze. We were the ones who wiped those chips.

"How can we be sure you won't bring another army across the wall?" demands Prince Otho.

"We're here to offer those assurances—" starts Sentin, but the imperator cuts him off with an irritated grunt.

"If you insist on discussing these things now, we may as well start dinner."

Instantly, one of the uniformed waiters steps forward. "This way, please."

The waiter opens a door and ushers us into a dining room. A long table that looks designed to seat at least two dozen people is set with eight place settings, all well apart from each other so we'll have to speak up to be heard.

Several more waiters join us. One pulls out a chair for me and holds it while I sit down, and others do the same for the rest. Then the waiters bustle around us, pouring us fresh drinks, although our old drinks are virtually untouched.

They bring out platters of food from a door that must lead into a kitchen, and one spoons some of it onto the plate in front of me. The food smells delicious, but looks nothing like what I'm used to. I stare down at some green leaves that must have been picked straight from a plant and coated in some kind of liquid. A thick white tube rests beside it, with something brown and chunky on the side. I can't wait to taste it all, but I sit patiently while everyone is served.

Prince Otho is sitting opposite me, and on the wall behind him is a portrait of his father, and an older man with the same beaky nose, who must be his grandfather. They were both imperators, so I guess Prince Otho is next in line to take over.

When the imperator picks up his knife and fork, I take it as an invitation to eat. Carefully, I spear one of the green leaves and push it in my mouth. Its flavor is incredible. As is everything else. I can barely stop myself from gobbling everything on my plate.

I'm in the process of devouring my dinner when I look up and catch the imperator watching me. The story Sentin told us runs through my mind, about the boy who ate gold-enfruit and grew roots. The imperator probably thinks after we've eaten his delicious food, we'll feel more like being generous.

Holding his gaze, I put my knife and fork down, and swallow what's in my mouth.

The imperator's gaze moves deliberately to Sentin. "What exactly do you want from us?" he asks abruptly. "I assume you're going to ask for something in exchange for peace."

Sentin nods. "Triton would like to import some of Deiterra's produce, and export its goods to you."

"Trade?" The imperator sounds incredulous, as though it's the most ridiculous demand he's ever heard.

Sentin inclines his head. "Trade," he agrees.

"First you destroy our grain stores, and now you want the rest of our food?"

"Our factories manufacture enough food in Triton to supply you with—"

"You're suggesting we eat chemicals?" The imperator's lip curls. The legates stay silent, but their expressions make it clear they're as revolted as their boss. The only one who doesn't look disgusted at the idea is Prince Otho.

"The food being produced in Triton's factories is nutritious—"

"Manufacturing food in test tubes goes against the principles Deiterra was founded on." The imperator makes a disgusted sound, spraying saliva over the table. "My father would roll in his grave."

"It would be a temporary solution until your grain store was replenished." Sentin sounds as unruffled as ever. "And new technology is being developed in Triton that I believe could be of great benefit to Deiterra."

"What kind of technology?" Prince Otho leans forward, his eyes alight with interest.

"Plant fertilization is your farmers' most labor-intensive task. Have you considered creating bees to do it for you?"

"Creating bees? You mean, engineering them in a lab?"

Sentin nods. "Our scientists grew a sabre-toothed tiger from ancient DNA traces found in fossils. They can certainly bring bees back into the world. And they can make them resistant to the toxins that drove them to extinction."

Prince Otho turns to his father and widens his eyes.

The imperator looks far less impressed. "If Triton has the answer to every problem, it must be a delightful place to live." He folds his arms in front of him. "So why do you want our food?"

"Triton is overcrowded, as you well know."

"Well you can't send all your people here," snaps the imperator. The legates all nod, agreeing with their boss.

"I'm not suggesting that." Sentin puts his elbows on the table, lacing his fingers together over his plate. "I'm simply suggesting we enjoy closer relations for our mutual benefit. In order to do that, we'll need to relax some restrictions around entry. We'll repair the wall, but install a proper gate for easier access. Our scientists will help Deiterra become more productive, and your growers will export a portion of their goods."

"Never." The imperator slams his hand down on the table, making all the plates and glasses jump. "You can't have our food. We only have enough to feed ourselves."

"When you have access to our technology, you'll produce a lot more food. Your country will prosper and your citizens will—"

"That's enough." The imperator scrapes his chair back and stands up. "My answer is no. My appetite has gone, and I won't entertain this discussion any longer." His legates put their cutlery down and stand up too.

"Please don't leave." Sentin swivels in his chair. "We have a lot to discuss."

"We have nothing to discuss." The imperator fixes his son with a pointed look. "Otho?"

The prince stands up slowly, his expression reluctant. "That was quick," he mutters.

"Your terms are unacceptable." The imperator glares at Sentin, then at me and Cale. "You will reconsider your offer before we speak again tomorrow. We will not agree to trade, we refuse your chemicals, and your scientists are not welcome here." He turns and sweeps out, followed by the legates.

"My apologies," says Prince Otho. "I thought the bees were a good idea." He nods at us and goes after his father.

When it's just Cale, Sentin and I left at the table, I let out a loud sigh. "That didn't go well."

"His behaviour could be a negotiating tactic." Sentin picks up his knife and fork and cuts a mouthful of food. But though he's making an effort to act like nothing is wrong, his body is tense and his shoulders have lifted. I'm either getting better at reading him, or he's finding it harder to hide his emotions. Maybe being in Deiterra is bringing old, buried tensions closer to the surface.

"So he didn't mean any of that?" asks Cale. He's sitting on the other side of the table, and like me, he's almost cleaned his plate. Sentin is beside me, and still has half his meal left.

Sentin lifts his fork, but doesn't take a bite. "Negotiations will resume tomorrow. I'll present my offer again, and eventually he'll accept."

Cale raises his eyebrows. "You sure? He seems to think our food is toxic and our scientists have cloven hooves and forked tongues."

"Maybe he's right about our food being toxic. Deiterran food tastes nothing like it." I put the last of my dinner into my mouth and try to chew slowly. "It's delicious," I mumble with my mouth full.

"Why are you so set on trading with Deiterra?" Cale frowns at Sentin. "And don't try to tell me it's for the joy of sharing this amazing food with Tritoners, because I don't believe you."

"Trade is the first step in a very long journey."

I'm expecting Sentin to say more, but his eyes have gone distant as though he's deep in thought.

Cale and I exchange a long, meaningful glance, having an entire silent conversation in which we both share our mutual frustration over having to drag information out of Sentin piece by piece.

"And...?" I prompt.

Sentin focuses on me. "My eventual goal is for the wall to come down, and for Deiterra and Triton to be a single nation. The first step is a gate in the wall, to facilitate trade. Information will flow through that gate, and common ground will be found. Our communities will become more alike. Eventually, the wall will be seen as an unnecessary hindrance."

"How long will all that take?" I ask.

He gives me one of his slow blinks. "Why do you persist in thinking the duration is important?"

"Years?" I ask. "Decades?"

"While somebody uses a Skin, their human body can be kept in a form of stasis. Assuming the Skin is regularly maintained, its user could live for centuries."

"Centuries?" Cale coughs out the word. "You can't seriously be planning that far ahead?"

"To achieve an ambitious outcome, it's necessary to maintain a high vantage point."

I lean forward, meeting Sentin's eyes, and speak in a low, determined voice so he knows my words are a warning. "But I don't like the view from up there. Not if you can't see Old Triton."

He cocks his head. "Old Triton wasn't kind to you, though, was it? When we met, you wore your defiance like armor. Underneath it, your fear was strong enough I could have detected it even without the sensors in my glasses."

"That's not true," I protest. He holds my gaze, and my face heats. "Showing fear only attracts sharks," I mutter.

"When you're subjected to a dangerous situation over a long period of time, it can rewire your brain to create permanent trauma. I was interested to see how using a Skin reversed that trauma."

I scratch my cheek before I realize what I'm doing. My cheek doesn't itch, because this Skin doesn't have any scars. It's just that talking about my old life is making me uncomfortable.

"You and I have always been outsiders." Sentin is still focused on me. "But that's a strength, not a weakness.

Embrace the power your new Skin gives you. Don't cling to old feelings toward Old Triton, or try to reverse past wrongs. Take a step back, and you'll realize a greater perspective only comes with distance."

"What are you saying?" Cale sounds annoyed.

When I drag my gaze from Sentin's and my eyes land on Cale's perfect New Triton face, it hits me how right Sentin is about having been an outsider. I'm the opposite of Cale. He fits in everywhere, and gets on with everyone. He once told me he'd never been in a fight. But I bet Sentin's been in plenty.

Cale gives Sentin a puzzled frown. "Are you trying to say that Old Triton doesn't matter?"

Sentin turns to Cale, and his expression shifts almost imperceptibly, all trace of emotion smoothing away. He's the one with armor, not me. But maybe Cale was right about him being willing to let me in, and give me a glimpse of whatever he's hiding.

"I'm merely suggesting we evaluate events dispassionately." His tone goes bland. "We should ensure our affiliations don't color our perception of the facts."

Cale opens his mouth, then closes it again, unable to argue.

I don't say anything either, because Sentin's words are going around and around in my head. He's right about my fear. I lived on a razor's edge for years, and my Leopard Skin freed me. Now, thanks to my new Skin, I'm both fearless *and* powerful.

Maybe he's right about everything. What did he say I was trying to do? Right past wrongs? Thinking about it that way, it seems like an impossible task. I mean, how can you change things that already happened? You can't, that's all. At some point, you have to move on.

I suck in a deep breath and blow it out in a loud rush of air.

From across the table, Cale shoots me a questioning look. Sentin is closer, and his eyes are on me too. But I get the idea he already knows exactly what I'm thinking.

TWELVE

Dinner is long over, and I'm in the room they gave me, lying in the darkness trying to sleep, when there's a knock at the door.

Cale. It must be him. Who else would knock so late at night?

I slip out of bed and cross quickly to the door, my pulse speeding up as I think of the night we spent together in the safe house. Pausing for a moment at the door, I smooth the knee-length shift I wore to bed and lift a hand to check my hair. I have no idea what kind of complicated technology keeps it looking so perfect, but my silky bob is as neat as always.

When I throw open the door, it's not Cale on the other side.

"Sentin?" I blink at him. He's still dressed in the smart black suit he wore to dinner, and the licorice and aniseed scent of his aftershave smells even better than before, as though freshly applied. He's as handsome as Cale, in his own way. Darker and more angular. Tall, and with an unevenness to his features that I've come to appreciate.

He inclines his head. "I'm going outside, and I'd like you to come with me."

"Outside?" I ask. "Where?"

"There's a bar within walking distance. You should see a little Deiterran nightlife while you're here."

I resist the urge to ask aloud whether I'm asleep and this is a weird dream. Sentin never does anything without a reason. If he wants me to go drinking with him at a Deiterran bar, then I'd better go. No matter how bizarre this is.

"Give me a minute to change."

I shut the door on him so I can slip into trousers, flat shoes, and a shirt. When I open it again, I ask, "Is this okay for where we're going?"

He holds out a strip of cloth. "Drape this over your hair."

I take it, frowning. "Why?"

"Because you don't look Deiterran."

Of course. I remember the hostile looks from the people who were working in the fields, and make a kind of hood with the fabric, pulling it forward at the sides so my face will be hard to see.

As Sentin leads me down the hall, I wonder about stopping to get Cale. But Sentin walks past the door to Cale's room, and I think better of it. Cale looks as foreign here as I do. Besides, my best guess about why we're going out is that Sentin needs to talk to me privately. Maybe he's worried there are listening devices here, and we'll be overheard. Although after our dinner conversation, it's a little late to worry about that.

"Will the Deiterrans mind us leaving like this?" I ask.

"Why should they mind? We're just going to enjoy ourselves."

I raise my eyebrows at him, doubting that Sentin's ever

gone to a bar to have fun in his life. There's definitely something clandestine going on.

At least he seems to know his way around the palace. He leads me down several long hallways, and manages to find the front entrance with no problem. There are two legionnaires stationed at the door. To my surprise, he takes my hand and tucks it into his arm before we walk up to them.

"We're going to a bar for a drink. We'll be back in an hour or two." His tone is more casual than I've ever heard it.

The legionnaires both salute. "Yes, sir. We'll call you a car."

"No need. It's a pleasant evening for a walk."

"Sir, our safety protocols—"

"We'd like to stay unaccompanied. I take full responsibility for our safety." Sentin leads me out the door, keeping his hand over mine, so I have to keep hold of his arm. To the legionnaires, we must look like lovers, which I assume is what he wants them to think.

I wouldn't have thought the imperator would let us walk out the door like this, but as we stroll down the grand driveway, nobody tries to stop us.

Tall, ornate lamps illuminate our path. The street in front of the house isn't lit up, but I guess it doesn't need to be when it's basically deserted. There are a few houses with lights on, and the occasional car drives past, but compared to Triton, it's a ghost town.

Sentin keeps hold of my arm while we walk, not letting it go even when we're out of sight of the palace. I look around curiously, my vision sharp in spite of the darkness. Besides, it's not really dark here, not compared to the oppressive black of an Old Triton night. The moon and stars are incredibly bright. Even brighter than they are in New Triton.

It's cool tonight, and I shiver, wishing I'd worn a warmer shirt. When the sun goes down at this time of year, it can get cold. But it's not winter yet, so at least we won't freeze. At least, we wouldn't in Triton.

"Where are we going?" I ask eventually, when Sentin doesn't volunteer any information.

He shoots a quick glance behind us. "Speak softly, and don't look over your shoulder. The legionnaires are following us, but we should pretend we don't know they're there."

I resist an overwhelming urge to look back at them. "Okay."

"We're going to find out what happened to the knights, because the swarm network has gone offline."

"What?" A fresh chill runs down my spine. I haven't checked whether my band is working, but if the knight's network is down, it can't be. "You can't contact them? What do you think's happened?"

"That's what we're going to find out."

"If we're being followed, how are we going to get to the knights without the imperator knowing?"

"We're going to the bar first, then we'll lose them. It's just up here."

Sure enough, there's a building ahead with a couple of empty tables outside on the sidewalk. A sign over the door says *Have A Rusty Nail*. I'm not sure if it's the name of the bar, an invitation to try a type of drink, or a threat of violence. Maybe all three.

Inside, soft, unfamiliar music is playing. I've never actually been inside a bar, but this place looks a little like New

Triton bars I've seen on the holo. It's a medium-sized room filled with tables and chairs, and there are some booths against the wall. At the back of the room is a counter with tall stools lined up against it. A woman is wiping glasses behind the counter, presumably keeping busy seeing as she's not serving drinks. There are less than a dozen people sitting at the tables, which doesn't seem like many for the size of the place. I check their faces, just in case Tori's here. A long shot, at best.

The bar is dimly lit, and small flickering lights on the tables give it a homely atmosphere. After doing a quick scan, I keep my head down so my headscarf hides my face. The people in here are ignoring us anyway, probably assuming we're just two more regular customers.

Sentin drops my arm and walks to the counter. "Hello, Bayley."

The woman's eyes widen. She puts down the glass she was wiping and drops her cloth on top of it. "Sentin. You look exactly the same." She shakes her head. "I should know by now that you always do what you say, but I didn't think you'd actually turn up. Not after all these years."

Then she turns her gaze to me, and frowns at the part of my face that's showing. She's around Sentin's age and pretty, but in an untweaked Old Triton kind of way. Not like me. With my deep, rich chestnut skin, sleek bob, and smooth, ageless face, I must look like an alien to her.

"Who's this?" Her eyes narrow.

"Some legionnaires are following us," he says.

"No shit." She's still staring at me. "You're from Triton?"

I nod. "My name is... Felicity. It's nice to meet you." It's the first time I've introduced myself with the president's first name, and it feels awkward on my tongue. Like the first time I said I was Rayne.

She doesn't reply. Her expression isn't hostile, but it's guarded. I can see that she's wondering what I'm doing here, and whether my presence will be a danger to her.

"We're going to sit in the far booth, the one you can't see into from outside," says Sentin. "We'll have a drink, make them think we're settling in. Then, after you bring us a second one, we'll slip out through the back door."

Bayley tilts her head, her lips thinning. "I haven't seen you in ten years, and instead of a proper hello, you expect me to bring you drinks, then clear a path to the back door for you? Nobody uses that door. There are boxes piled in front of it."

"I apologize for being abrupt, but if we talk for too long, the legionnaires will realize we know each other. It's better if that doesn't happen."

"Sorry," I mutter, giving her an apologetic look. I don't know their history, but it seems like Sentin's asking an awful lot from her, especially seeing as she probably has plenty of reasons to hate Tritoners. And Sentin isn't exactly asking nicely.

She shakes her head. "Same old Sentin. The years haven't changed you a bit, have they? Fine, I'll clear the path to the door but you have to help me move the boxes."

"Thank you, Bayley. And please, would you serve two drinks to the booth? Give us anything, so long as they look alcoholic, but aren't."

Bayley shoots another narrow-eyed look at me. "Make sure you keep your face covered. I don't want trouble."

Sentin leads me to a booth, and we sit on either side of the table. The flickering lights I'd noticed on the tables are actually candles, nestled in glass cases.

Bayley comes over with two small glasses filled with a clear liquid, and puts them in front of us. "So, that's it, then?" She fists her hands on her hips. "Now you want me to start clearing a path to the back door?"

"I'm sorry about the circumstances." He hesitates. "In spite of our haste, it's good to see you, Bayley."

"Yeah." She sighs. "Nice to see you too, Sentin. I only wish you were here to catch up, instead of using me to dodge some legionnaires."

His brow creases, and his eyes are dark. He looks genuinely upset that he's upset her. "As I said, we're pressed for time. But here." He digs something out of his pocket and hands it to her.

She wrinkles her nose at it like it's nasty, and puts the object back on the table. "Keep it. I don't actually need it. Not that you'd know how I'm doing, but I'm fine, thanks for asking."

The thing she's put down is a metal coin. I get a jolt of recognition. It doesn't look exactly like the coin my father gave me before he died, but it's close.

"I'm sorry, Bayley." Sentin's mouth twists, and he looks more uncomfortable than I've ever seen him. "If the legionnaires weren't at the door, we could talk. As it is, we'll have to save it for next time."

"Fine." She turns to leave, then hesitates and turns back. "On second thought, I may as well keep this. I figure I deserve it, and you don't use money in Triton anyway, right?" She picks up the coin and tosses it in one hand. "Do you know Julius and Newport both died? I mean, not that you'll be sad, after the way they treated you. But I thought you should know. When the wall came down, they rushed to fight against the knights."

"I didn't know. Thank you for telling me."

"Lots of people died, but I..." Shaking her head, she shoves both hands aggressively into the pockets of her jeans. "Like I said, they gave you no reason for you to cry for them."

"I'm sorry for your loss." His tone is careful.

Bayley turns quickly on her heel, stalks back to the bar, and slips through a door behind it.

Sentin's gaze drops to his drink. He studies it, his eyes distant, as if he's too deep in thought to actually drink it. I take a sip of mine. It's just as delicious as I'm coming to expect. In fact, it tastes a little like one of the fruits I tried.

I'm burning to know who the woman is, but instead of asking, I just give him a pointed look with my eyebrows raised. If the silence drags on for long enough, maybe he'll get tempted to fill it.

It doesn't work. Of course. After sipping my drink and holding in my questions for what seems like forever, I have to speak up.

"Who is she?" I ask.

He lets out a long breath. "My cousin."

"The daughter of your father's... brother? Sister?"

"Does it matter?"

"I'm interested in your family, and what your life was like over here."

The flickering candle casts stark shadows on Sentin's face, and makes his eyes even harder to read than normal. It also highlights his elegant features. I finally understand why he doesn't look overly tweaked, because they don't seem to have tweaking in Deiterra. But I like that his features are mostly natural. It makes me feel closer to him, somehow, even though he's closed off and secretive.

"My life in Deiterra was difficult," he says in his slow, precise way. "I was always regarded as a Tritoner. As a foreigner. Much the same way I was treated when I returned to Triton."

"Who were the people Bayley mentioned? The ones who were killed?"

"Her brothers. The four of us were brought up together, though they objected to my presence. They thought I should have stayed in Triton."

My heart constricts. Maybe there's a reason Sentin never wants to show any emotion. Perhaps it was beaten out of him. There were people at the shelter like that, hollow-eyed, and carved out inside. People who'd used up all their fear and had nothing left.

"Sounds rough." I don't try to keep my sympathy out of my voice.

He looks back down at the candle's dancing flame. "Your childhood must have been rougher. I had plenty to eat, and I spent my days learning."

"My life only got hard after my father died. Before that, we lived in an apartment, and I went to school. Most of my early memories are good ones." I don't mention that sometimes in the shelter, I used to curse those memories. The problem with having it so good and then losing it all, is being aware of exactly how far you've fallen.

"I have some good memories too. My schooling in Deiterra was problematic, but I liked going to university in Triton."

"You were bullied at school, as well as at home?"

He hesitates, lifting his drink and taking a sip before he answers. "I was an outsider, who found the lessons simplistic. That seemed to be a point of contention."

I can guess how it must have been. The other kids must have resented him showing them up.

I think I'm finally starting to understand Sentin. Like me, he wants to change the things that affected him most. For him, that's the divide between Deiterra and Triton, and I get why he wants to tear down the wall.

"I'm sorry you had to go through that." I have a strong urge to reach across the table and touch his hand, but I'm not sure how he'd respond. He'd probably look at me as though I'm crazy.

He puts his glass down. "Thank you. But your pity's misplaced. If I hadn't lived in Deiterra as a child, we wouldn't have been allowed to come here, and no treaty would be possible. The imperator has an extreme dislike of outsiders, and we're lucky he considers me enough of a Deiterran to let me bring you here." His tone is matter-of-fact, but I know his lack of expression is just a mask he puts on.

"Can I ask you something, Sentin? Why do the legionnaires call you sir?" I'm half expecting him to avoid the question, but his gaze stays direct as he answers.

"Because my father was the ambassador. Like most positions here, it's a hereditary title, and considered a military post. Therefore, I outrank the legionnaires who escorted us to Reliance."

I blink at him. "Hereditary title? Are you saying you're the new Deiterran ambassador?"

He gives a small shrug. "For years it's been a ceremonial position with no real power."

"Still. Why didn't I know you were the new ambassador?"

"It's not important. All his title did was grant my father

access to high-profile events in Triton that he wanted to attend."

"I guess you don't need a title to go anywhere, right? You're the president's right-hand man, and even if you weren't, I bet you'd find a way to get in wherever you wanted."

I drain the last of my drink, and right on cue, Bayley comes over with two more.

"The legionnaires are sitting at one of the outside tables, trying to be inconspicuous." She places our drinks in front of us. "How are you going to leave without them seeing you?"

"Go out and ask if you can take their order. While they're distracted, we'll sneak behind the bar."

She puts her hands on her hips. "You'll owe me, Sentin. Even more than you owe me now, I mean. I cleared enough space for you to get to the door, except for the heaviest boxes."

He digs in his pocket for another coin, but stops when she flicks one hand in a dismissive gesture. "I'm not talking about money, stupid. You're so *literal*."

I suppress a smile. Judging from her insult, they must have been close. At least Sentin had one friend here.

"Then I'll owe you a favor," he says.

"I'd settle for a proper catch up, sometime when you're not running from the legion."

His shoulders drop a little, as though the tension is ebbing out of him, and I finally realize he must have been nervous about seeing her. He nods, and for the first time, a ghost of a smile crosses his lips. "I'd like that, Bayley. I promise, if I can find a way to make it happen, I will."

"I'll hold you to it." She nods at him, then me, and heads outside to speak to the legionnaires.

Sentin watches her go. A few moments later, he motions for me to follow and scoots out from the booth, crouching low. We dash behind the bar, then through the door to a little storage area filled with bottles on shelves and in cartons. He pushes his way through the cartons, then shifts a couple out of the way to reveal an old, rusted door that's obviously never used.

The lock turns with a harsh, reluctant sound, and Sentin throws his weight into forcing the old hinges to open. We step through the gap into a small, foul-smelling back alley, and when we're through, he pushes the door shut behind us.

"This way." He takes off down the alley, running silently, faster than I would have expected. Because he's so smart, I hadn't expected him to be athletic, but I suppose his lean body is probably well suited for running long distances.

We stick to dark roads, but then again, for all I know, the whole of Deiterra might be this dark and quiet at night. Sentin seems to know where he's going, so I just put my head down and follow, keeping the headscarf pulled over my face and sticking to the deepest shadows in case anyone happens to glance out from a window.

Funny, I used to stand out because of my scars, not because my face was too perfect.

Sentin stops to peer around the corner of a building. "It's just ahead."

"What is? The barracks?" I whisper.

He shakes his head. "The knights aren't in the barracks."

"If they're not answering when you call, how do you know where they are?"

"Each has a tracking device."

"So they went silent, then they moved? That doesn't sound good."

"Come on." He slips around the corner, keeping low and close to the building. This street is just as dark as all the others, but instead of cute houses with gardens, it's lined with ugly block buildings. They're all dark and quiet, and I assume they're buildings where people work, rather than homes.

Sentin stops outside one of them and peers in its front window. Then he tiptoes down the side of the building, looking into every window he comes to, and testing them to see if they'll open. At the rear of the building, there's only a narrow gap between the building and a high brick wall. The windows on this side are smaller.

He stops beside one and takes off the light jacket he's wearing.

"What are you doing?" I whisper.

"I'll break the glass." He starts winding the cloth around his hand.

"You've already been injured by broken glass." I take the jacket from him, though the wound on his hand is healing well. "Let me do it. I'm stronger, and I don't cut easily."

Using the jacket to cover my fist, I punch out the glass. The noise seems much louder than it should be, because the night is so silent.

I drape the jacket over the windowsill in case there are slivers of glass, and give Sentin a boost up. He scrambles inside, and I follow, dropping lightly inside a small room that's pitch black. It looks like a storage room, lined with shelves. It's only because my vision is so good that I can make out the door.

I turn the handle slowly and ease the door open. The

hallway outside is silent, and almost as dark. The building *feels* empty. I can't hear any movement.

Sentin must be thinking the same thing, because he touches a switch and a light flickers on in the hallway. Rooms come off it on either side, their doors all open. The only closed door is at the far end. Stepping forward, I peer into the first room.

A familiar sight sends a chill down my spine. It's some kind of laboratory.

A trolley has medical instruments laid out on it, next to a long table that holds a lot of other equipment. I recognise a microscope, but little else.

Sentin steps into the room and looks into a glass cabinet in the corner. He opens it, and cold air blasts out, along with a terrible smell. It's a fridge, and whatever in there has gone bad.

He pulls out a dish. "They didn't get all the tissue out," he murmurs.

I move next to him, and frown at the mass of circuitry in the dish. Some has bits of meat embedded in it. My stomach starts churning, and not just because of the horrible stench coming from it. "Is that part of a Skin's brain? Is it what happened to the knights we brought with us?"

He shakes his head. "It's older than that. The brain matter has long decayed." He puts the dish back and closes the fridge door. "Come on."

In the next lab, we find a knight's dismembered arms and hands. In the next, its legs. Each room has more parts, but together they must make only two or three knights, at the most.

In the last few labs, we find bigger machinery that barely fits into the small lab rooms, and reminds me of the manufacturing equipment I worked with in the factory.

"They're trying to manufacture their own Skins," explains Sentin. He turns on a bright overhead lamp, then uses a pair of tweezers to pick up a chip. "Not functional yet," he mutters. Frowning he peers more closely at the chip. "I'll need to put this under a microscope to be sure, but they're closer than I thought they'd be to duplicating our technology. This part of it, at least." He brings his gaze up to meet mine. His usual mask has dropped away. His brow is creased, and his expression troubled. "I'd considered it unlikely they'd be this far advanced. They must have a source of information I hadn't factored into my calculations. Perhaps some help from a scientist involved in the Skin program."

"They can create their own Skin army?" I ask.

"Not yet. But soon."

I swallow, imagining the carnage if that happened. We'd have to rebuild our own Skin army to hold them back. It would be the Skin Hunter contest all over again, but on an epic scale, with hundreds or thousands of Skins. Whatever battleground they fought on would be destroyed, along with any civilians caught in the crossfire.

"Where are the knights we brought with us?" I ask.

"There's only one more place left to look." He puts the chip down and we move to the closed door at the end of the hall.

I'm in front of Sentin, so I'm the one who slowly opens the door. My eyes focus on what's inside, and I jerk backward, my heart racing. The room's full of people.

But of course it isn't.

I drag in a deep breath, then push the door fully open so the light from the hall shines in. The room is full of knights, not people. They're all standing perfectly still. I step inside and check all the Skins, searching for...

There he is. One knight has a bright yellow stain on his armored hand, and my gut clenches. It's Clayton.

Sentin is busy examining one of the other Skins. "No visible damage," he says. "That means their chips were wiped. They must have developed a method to erase data from the internal chip from a distance. Perhaps they used a sonic pulse, but the equipment in the labs suggested it was a directional weapon. We need to do a more intensive search of the building."

"Now they have forty-seven more Knight Skins. We've already given them a ready-made army."

"Not yet. They're missing an important piece of the puzzle." He lifts one hand to tap the back of his neck.

"Our chips. They don't have any to copy?" I lift my own hand to touch my neck. "The one in your human body's different to the ones in the Skins?"

He nods. "It's complicated to explain, but in a sense, one is the controller."

"They know we have chips. You and Cale, anyway, because you were in the Skin Hunter contest. And they probably think I have one too. What's to stop them cutting us open and extracting our chips?"

Sentin turns toward the door. "They won't do that until we've outlived our usefulness as hostages."

"What?" I go after him, putting my hand on his arm to stop him. "We're hostages?"

"Without the knights to protect us, we're at their mercy."

"Then we need to get Cale and go back to Triton." I swallow, thinking of Tori. I have no idea how to find her, but how can I leave without trying?

He shakes his head. Although he sounds calm, his gray eyes are as hard as iron. "Not without negotiating a peace treaty. It's vital we do that now. If we leave, communication will cease and another war is inevitable."

"How are we going to negotiate a peace treaty when they're holding all the cards?"

Sentin sweeps his gaze around the knights and his jaw tightens. "We'll find a way."

THIRTEEN

The next morning, I'm awake early and seated at the table in the imperator's fancy dining room before Cale or Sentin appears. Breakfast is a selection of pancakes and fruit laid out for us to help ourselves. It smells good and probably tastes just as delicious as dinner did, but I feel as enthusiastic about eating it as if it were the bland stew spat out by the machines in the shelter.

It doesn't help that there's a waiter standing by the door who's supposedly there to make sure we have everything we need, but who's standing in a military pose and looks suspiciously like a guard.

We're hostages. If the imperator decides to carve one or more of us up for our chips, the only thing going for us is that I'm a lot stronger than they'll expect me to be. But the wall is quite a distance from here. Even if we made it out of the palace, I doubt we'd get all the way to Triton before they stopped us.

Cale eventually joins me at the table. "The knights must have changed the access settings for their swarm network," he says as he piles his plate up with food. "I can't connect."

He obviously has no idea about what happened last night. I force myself to wait until he's had time to enjoy some breakfast before murmuring the entire story in his ear. When I've finished, his face is pale, and he pushes his plate away. Like me, he's lost his appetite.

"We should have made a break for it," he says quietly, echoing my thoughts.

When Sentin comes in, he nods a greeting, his expression serious. He serves himself a plate of food, and sits opposite me.

"What now?" asks Cale in a low voice. "Do you have a way to get us out of this mess?"

I wait anxiously for him to say that he does. After having all night to think about it, surely he's figured out some clever way to turn the tables.

But Sentin hesitates, his brows drawing together. "Do you trust me?" he asks after a moment.

Cale and I exchange a confused look. Then I nod. "I trust you," I murmur, surprised to realize that it's true.

Cale nods too, though he doesn't look so sure.

"I need you both to make a promise," says Sentin. "It's vital the peace treaty is negotiated. We need to continue pushing for the deal I've proposed, no matter what happens."

"What do you think might happen?" My sense of dread is growing.

He picks up his knife and fork, glancing at the waiter who's still standing to attention by the door. "Promise you'll sign a peace treaty, no matter what. This is important."

"Why do we need to promise?" Cale narrows his eyes. "What are you planning?"

Sentin cuts a neat slice in the pancakes, but doesn't make any move to lift the food to his mouth. He's waiting for an answer.

"Fine," I say impatiently. "We promise. Just tell us your plan."

Cale leans forward, his gaze fixed on Sentin. "This isn't the time for secrets."

Sentin glances at the waiter again and his voice drops even lower. "It's neither the time nor place to speak openly."

I can't help but glance at the portraits hanging on the wall behind him. The imperator is staring down at us. No wonder I feel like we're being watched.

A muscle ticks in Cale's jaw. "Just tell us. I hate sitting around like this, when I don't have any idea what's going to happen."

Sentin lifts his fork. "I doubt we'll be sitting around for long."

The words are barely out of his mouth when the door flies open and the imperator sweeps in. He's wearing a long red robe and an impressive scowl. Behind him are the legates we met last night, all three of them frowning. The imperator's son isn't far behind them. Otho is the most sympathetic of the Deiterrans we've met so far, but even he looks stern this morning.

The imperator fixes Sentin and me with a glare. "Where did you go last night?" he demands.

"To a bar. We had a pleasant drink and enjoyed some music." Sentin puts a forkful of food in his mouth and chews.

"You fled the bar through its back door."

Sentin swallows. "President Morelle wanted to see a little more of Deiterra." His eyebrows go up, as though he's surprised. "We had no idea you were tracking our movements."

"For well over an hour, you were unaccounted for. Where were you?"

"Walking. It was a pleasant evening and the streets were nice and quiet."

The imperator lets out an exasperated breath. "Very well, we'll try this a different way." He turns to the two legionnaires who followed them all in, and are standing ramrod-straight next to the door. "Bring in the other one."

One of the legionnaires nods and slips out. The other stands even straighter.

Sentin moves his gaze to me and I frown back a silent question. *The other one?* As usual, his expression is unreadable, and Cale looks as confused as I am.

A few moments later, the legionnaire comes back, pulling someone along with him. She looks spitting mad, and snatches her arm out of the legionnaire's grip as soon as she's inside the door.

Tori.

I open my mouth to say her name, then clamp my jaw shut. She doesn't know who I really am. To her, I'm the enemy.

Cale leaps to his feet. "Tori! Are you okay? Did they hurt you?"

Her eyes widen as he moves to her side, and her mouth drops open with surprise. "What are you doing here?"

"We're here to negotiate a peace treaty." Sentin's voice is loud enough to cut across everyone else. He and I are still sitting at the dining table. His gaze is focused on the imperator, addressing him instead of Tori. "We would like to continue those discussions."

The imperator folds his arms, glaring down his nose at

Sentin. "This is no longer a negotiation. I will inform you of the terms of our agreement, and you'll accept those terms. If you don't agree, I'll demonstrate what will happen to all of you." He nods at Tori. "I'll start with this Tritoner, who crossed illegally into our country, and is therefore subject to the strictest penalty under our laws. She'll be executed without trial."

Cale draws in a sharp breath, and I can see the effort it takes him not to shout a protest. By his side, Tori stares open-mouthed at the imperator, her face pale. She's wearing clean, Deiterran-style clothing, and looks healthy, so at least they don't seem to have been mistreating her.

Tori's gaze goes to Prince Otho, and her expression changes. She frowns at him, and he gives his head an almost imperceptible shake.

"What exactly are your terms?" asks Sentin.

The imperator's arrogant stare moves to me. "President Morelle will immediately resign, appointing me as her replacement. I will be both Imperator of Deiterra, and President of Triton."

Sentin doesn't look surprised, let alone shocked. "In Triton, we have democratic elections," he says. "The presidential election will be held in—"

"Not anymore." The imperator flicks a dismissive hand. "Triton is now under my control."

"Never!" Cale glares at the imperator.

"That's a little presumptuous." There's no hint of anger in Sentin's voice. If anything, he sounds mildly amused. "You've never set foot in Triton, yet you'd like to control it?"

"I have your president," snarls the imperator. "She'll do what I tell her."

"Have you forgotten we have forty-seven knights we can call on?"

I manage not to gape at Sentin, but it takes an effort to keep my mouth closed and my expression neutral. Cale's eyes widen, but he also has his jaw clamped shut.

The imperator smirks, and behind him his legates all fail to hide smug smiles. The only one whose expression doesn't change is Otho. My guess is that he doesn't know his father has wiped the Skins' chips.

"Have you tried calling your knights?" asks the imperator.

"Of course. And I know that you think you've deactivated them. However, I can reactivate them whenever I wish."

The imperator scoffs. "That's impossible. We erased the knights' connections with their human operators."

"Very well. Then I'll make you a deal." Sentin stands up. "Take me to the place you're keeping the knights, and I'll reactivate them while you watch. If I succeed, you'll agree to the terms I've proposed for our peace treaty. If I fail, the president will resign."

I stand too, still not sure what Sentin's playing at, but wanting to back him up. There's no way he can reactivate the knights once their chips have been wiped. Can he?

The imperator narrows his eyes. "Your knights are dead. They won't come back to life."

Sentin cocks his head. "But if they have that functionality, don't you want to know about it?"

The imperator stares at Sentin a moment longer, then gives a sharp nod. "The president will accompany us. When your knights fail to reactivate, she will immediately record her resignation to be broadcast to Triton." He motions to Cale and Tori. "Your two compatriots will remain here, under guard. If you refuse to comply, they'll both become subject to our laws, and be executed as illegal immigrants."

Sentin nods. "Agreed."

I clench my jaw, forcing myself to stay silent. There'd better be a damn good reason Sentin's willing to use Cale and Tori's lives as bargaining chips.

The imperator turns and sweeps toward the door. His legates follow.

Otho hesitates, looking at Tori. "This isn't what I wanted," he murmurs so softly that only my enhanced hearing lets me pick it up. "I'm sorry. I promise, I'll do whatever I can."

I don't get to hear what Tori says back to him, because the legionnaires step forward, motioning me to follow the imperator and his staff. Sentin strides out ahead of me without looking back.

I hesitate, wishing I had a moment longer so I could speak privately to Cale and Tori. If the imperator makes good on his threat, this could be the last time I ever see them. I only wish I weren't in this Skin. I want to let Tori know I'm not a stranger, and say goodbye to Cale as *me*, instead of somebody he hates.

"Come on, Madam President." Prince Otho's voice is gentle. "There's no point resisting."

The legionnaires take my arms to escort me out, and I crane my neck around to get one last look at Cale and Tori before I let them pull me out the door.

Cale stretches his hand toward me, his expression stricken. He starts mouthing something, but the door closes before I can tell what he's saying.

Once in the hallway, the legionnaires let go of my arms, but stay on either side of me. With them as my shadows, I can't talk to Sentin to ask what he's planning. More legionnaires march in front of the imperator and his legates, as well as behind me. If I fight back, I might not be able to overpower them all, and I'd put Cale and Tori's lives at risk.

Outside the palace, cars are waiting for us. As we drive to the building we visited last night, I stare sightlessly out the window, trying to figure out what Sentin could possibly have planned. But by the time we pull up to it, I'm no closer to an answer.

In daylight, the squat buildings on this street look a little depressing. The legionnaires run ahead to hold the front doors open, then we all file through, surprising several white-coated workers in the building's small entrance. "Your Excellency," they chorus, bowing low to the imperator and Prince Otho.

The imperator waves them all aside, barely slowing down. He knows exactly where he's going as he leads us to the room Sentin and I visited last night. And when his legionnaires throw open the door, I see the same thing I did then. All our knights are standing still and quiet. They haven't moved, of course. Their chips have all been wiped.

"Here are your knights," the imperator turns to Sentin with a cold smile curving his lips. "They're as dead as your compatriots will be, unless your president resigns."

Sentin starts into the room, then stops and turns back to the imperator as though he's just thought of something. "Would you like to invite your scientists to watch me bring the knights back to life? I can only do it once. I'm sure they won't want to miss it."

The imperator studies him, his expression suspicious. "Very well," he says at last. He turns to one of his legionnaires and gives him an order. The man hurries off, presumably to find the scientists in charge of the place.

"Come in." Sentin opens the door wide, beckoning the imperator and his legates into the cramped room.

Otho's face drops as he stares into the small space, and he tugs uncomfortably at the neck of his shirt. "I'll wait out here." He steps backward, and I remember what he said about being claustrophobic. "I can see perfectly well from the hallway."

Sentin nods. "It's a quick procedure. You won't need to wait long."

Four white-coated scientists approach the doors, craning their necks to try to see in past the press of people.

I move backward with Otto, wanting to give the legates and scientists as much space as possible. As strong as I am now, living in the shelter made me wary of letting strange people get too close. And if Sentin's plan fails, I may need to try and fight my way out of here. I can't imagine the knights coming back to life, but if Sentin really does have a way to make that happen, things could get messy. Whatever happens, I'm ready for anything.

The imperator seems to be the only one in the small room to have a small circle of respectful space around him. The legates and scientists jostle with each other, cramming in against the knights. Some legionnaires take up positions beside the door, standing to attention, the rest stand stiffly beside Otho and me, making the hallway almost as crowded as the room with the knights.

Otho's still tugging at his collar. "It's hot," he says. "Are you hot?" He turns to the legionnaires. "Stay here. We won't go far." He motions me to walk with him and we move further down the hallway, away from the room.

"As you know, the knights' chips are no longer functional." Sentin's voice drifts to me, muffled but easy to pick up with my sharp hearing. "However, one of the Skins holds the key to instantly restoring their coding. It's the instrument I'll use to bring them all back to life.

"Which Skin?" The imperator sounds impatient.

"A knight with new technology. It has a yellow stain on its hand."

Next to me, Otho asks quietly, "Can he really bring the knights back to life?'

"I don't know." I frown, listening harder for what's happening in the room. Why does Sentin want them to look for Clayton's Skin?

"This one has a yellow stain on its hand," says one of the legates. "But it's as dead as the others."

"Ah, that's the one. Do you see the markings on the back of its neck?" Sentin's voice is more muffled now. I assume he and the others are crowded around the knight, searching for markings that I'm pretty sure don't exist.

I have a very bad feeling about this. Whatever Sentin's up to, I don't see how it can possibly end well.

The prince shakes his head, looking as troubled as I feel. "Surely if there were new technology, you'd know about it, Madam President? It's hard to believe—"

With a deafening BOOM, the room Sentin's in explodes.

FOURTEEN

The force of the explosion knocks me and the prince backward, slamming us together against the wall. As we go sprawling, the heat from the fireball rolls over me. My ears ring.

I lie frozen for a moment. Stunned. Then I scramble to my feet, staring in horror at the fire that's engulfed the room. A fire nobody could survive.

But Sentin can't have blown himself up. There's no way he'd kill himself. He must still be alive.

"Father," croaks Otho. He's still on the floor, trying to pull himself up to standing. His face is red from the heat, and he looks as stunned as I am.

Water bursts from a sprinkler on the ceiling, a weak drizzle that sputters unevenly. Its coldness is a relief on my singed skin, but it's doing nothing to put out the flames. They're roaring even higher, and the heat is becoming more intense.

"Come on. We need to get out of here." I bend and help the prince to his feet, as several of his legionnaires drag themselves off the floor.

I let two of them push me away from the prince and take hold of him themselves to help him outside. One legionnaire keeps hold of my arm, dragging me with him though I'm perfectly capable of walking.

My brain is the only part of me that isn't working. I can't think straight. How could Sentin possibly have escaped that room? The fire is burning so fiercely, I can't imagine anyone making it out. But the alternative is impossible. Somehow, he must have escaped the flames.

Once on the sidewalk outside the building, I gulp in lungfuls of fresh air.

"Please excuse me, Prince Otho, but where is the imperator?" A legionnaire asks the question once and then again, as workers pour out of the burning building.

The prince's face is still mottled red, and his eyes are glassy. He stares at the ground, shaking his head, ignoring the legionnaire's questioning. He must be in shock. Either that, or his ears are ringing worse than mine, and he can't hear anything.

"I think they're dead," I tell the legionnaire. "The imperator and his legates were in the room that exploded."

The legionnaire stares at me with wide, horrified eyes. "Dead?" he repeats. "The imperator is dead?"

Around us, everyone starts murmuring, repeating the news. The sound quickly swells.

"What happened?" demands the legionnaire. "What caused the explosion?"

I shake my head. "I don't know. The room just went up in flames."

"A bomb? A booby trap?"

"I don't know."

The prince slowly lifts his head to stare at me. "You

must have known what would happen." His eyes narrow. "It was a trap. You and Sentin planned it."

"No, I swear, I had no idea. I'm as shocked as you are." The words sound breathless. My lungs are laboring because I can't quite catch my breath, and my hands are shaking. Nothing seems real. If I could untangle my thoughts, maybe I could figure out what just happened.

"Why should I believe you?" he demands.

"If I'd thought Sentin was planning to kill himself—" My voice breaks. Sentin's dead. He's really dead. I can't deny it any longer.

Which means the President's Skin is mine forever.

Wait. What am I thinking? I must be a terrible person to let a thought like that cross my mind now. Sentin's barely dead, and he was young and brilliant, and had his whole life ahead of him. More than that, he was my friend.

What kind of monster am I that my sorrow is tinged with relief?

"His promise to wake the knights was a lie," spits the prince. "It was just a trap."

I force my swirling emotions down so I can answer. "I didn't know what Sentin was doing, or why he was talking about the knights waking up. I thought maybe he'd developed a new technology."

"But you suspected he was lying?"

I squeeze my hands into fists to stop them trembling. "I wasn't sure. And if he was lying, I had no idea why."

"He wanted them all to get close, so they'd all be killed." The prince's mouth twists. "Our legionnaires searched you. How did Sentin get an explosive?"

"They didn't search us. Sentin assured them we had no weapons, and they accepted his word. So did I. You think I would have let him blow himself up if I had any clue that's what he was planning?"

A heavy weight presses against my chest, squeezing the air from my lungs. As impossible as it is to believe, Sentin's really gone.

Now I understand why he made me promise to negotiate a peace treaty. He knew he wouldn't be around to do it himself. But how can I possibly ask for peace after the imperator's murder?

"You killed my father," snaps the prince. "I should have you executed."

My head lifts at his harsh tone, and a flare of grief and anger ignites in my chest, strengthening my voice. "You could do that. But haven't we had enough killing?"

He lets out a furious sound. "You're the ones who waged war on *us*."

"Yes, and we were wrong to do that. Let's not make it worse."

"That's your argument for why I shouldn't have you shot?"

"It's my argument for why we need to negotiate a peace treaty. Together, we can stop any more senseless violence. Deiterra and Triton will both be better off."

For a moment, I dare to hope the prince might agree. He seems a reasonable man, far more reasonable than his father. Then his lips press together, and he lifts one hand to his eyes as though the enormity of what just happened has hit him again, even harder. His shock might sweep away all reason.

"We'll talk more about it later." He draws his hand back to his side and turns to the legionnaires. "Make sure everyone gets out of the building. Are the fire trucks and ambulances on their way?"

The closest legionnaire snaps a salute. "Yes, Your Excellency. They're almost here."

Prince Otho motions toward the crowd of scientists. "Get these people further away from the building. If the ambulances are delayed, you may use my cars to take the injured to the hospital."

"I can hear a fire truck, Your Excellency. The ambulances should be just behind it."

"Good. I want that fire out quickly, and all the captured Knight Skins salvaged. Have the knights moved to a secure location, and ensure the scientists can resume their work." He moves away, checking on the people who are still being carried out of the burning building.

I suck in a breath. My legs feel weak and I'd give anything to be able to sink to the ground and drop my head into my hands. If Sentin were here, he'd probably order me not to fall apart. I can imagine his calm voice telling me to remember what I'm here to do, that mourning the dead is a luxury I can't afford. Still, I can't stop the sick, miserable feeling that's constricting my chest and squeezing my insides.

Otho is directing the legionnaires to help the crowd. He's hiding his grief well.

Two legionnaires march over to me. "We're to take you back to the palace, ma'am."

I nod and let them put me in a car. Anyway, it's not like I have a choice, and the prince is busy. Better to let the shock wear off and talk to him later.

But the moment I'm in the car, sandwiched between two stern-faced legionnaires, I feel my composure slip, and the pressure on my chest becomes almost unbearable.

Was Sentin planning this all along?

Why was he willing to pay such a high price?

I wish I could convince myself he managed to somehow slip out of that room unhurt. It would be the world's best magic trick if he did.

Now my selfish relief has gone, replaced by a sense of loss so strong, I can hardly breathe. I'm never going to see him again.

I squeeze my eyes shut, my throat burning as I fight back tears. His handsome face is imprinted in my memory, the way he looked last night in the candlelight when he confessed his miserable childhood and my heart broke for him.

He was the invisible guiding force behind everything, the one with the plan, the genius who always had an opinion. Now he's gone, I feel lost.

What am I going to do without him?

FIFTEEN

Since Sentin's death, I've grown to hate the imperator's palace, mainly because I've been cooped up doing nothing for two days, confined to quarters while Otho decided whether or not I could be trusted. This is the first time the legionnaires have let me out of my room.

Now, I'm sitting on an upright wooden chair in one of the palace's luxurious sitting rooms. The two legionnaires who escorted me here said I've been summoned for an audience with Otho. They're standing by the door, their hands by their sides, staring straight ahead.

The door opens and Otho comes in, with Cale and Tori behind him.

Cale's face lights up when he sees me, and I'm so relieved to see them both, I want to jump up and hug them. Instead, I stand and duck my head in a respectful bow, keeping my gaze on Otho.

"Your Excellency," I say. My legionnaire guards haven't exactly been talkative, but one did tell me that the ceremonial transfer of power isn't yet complete and it'll be a few days before Otho officially becomes the new imperator. Still, it can't hurt to start using his title now.

Otho gives me the barest nod in return, and sits on the couch opposite me. Tori settles herself next to him. Cale leans against the wall next to the fireplace, and I sink back onto the hard wooden chair, debating what to say. Judging by the way Otho is staring at me with narrowed, suspicious eyes, he still hasn't made up his mind about me.

"Thank you for seeing me." I meet Otho's gaze. "I want to assure you again that I didn't know what Sentin was going to do. It shocked me as much as it did you."

"I have no way to know whether you're telling the truth." Otho's voice is clipped.

"You're right." I spread my hands, palms up. "You can choose whether to believe me or not. But really, your choice is whether or not you want to negotiate a peace treaty with Triton."

"Why should I negotiate with you?"

"Because you want the things I can offer," I say. "Food. Technology. Infrastructure. The same things Sentin talked about." I only wish I knew more about what Sentin wanted. I'm trying to keep my promise to him with only the bare fragments of information he gave me.

Otho grunts, sounding unconvinced. "Why shouldn't I do what my father wanted and use you as a hostage? I could get what I want without giving anything in return."

I nod. "You could threaten to kill me, but it won't work. If I die, the election will be brought forward so Triton can elect a new president. Nobody's going to try very hard to stop that happening, and I don't have any family who'll rush to save me."

Cale pushes himself off the wall, turning to face Otho. "The president's right. It wouldn't be a good long-term strategy. You'd get some food and supplies, but without heavy industry, you're crippled. What happens when your water tanks disintegrate? Or the last of your solar cells degrade? Do you have the resources to fix them?"

I stare at him in surprise. Don't the Deiterrans have any factories? Maybe their water and power systems were built before the wall went up. Or perhaps our soldiers torched their factories as well as their food supply.

Tori leans closer to Otho and pitches her voice low, as though she's here as his advisor. "If you make a deal, you could get everything you need."

"Your knights are dead." Otho doesn't take his eyes from me. "Without them, Triton is less of a threat. My army could invade."

"We still have more soldiers than you do," I point out. "Not that I want to use them. More fighting will get us nowhere."

"I used to make my living as a professional gamer." Cale walks over to the other couch in the room and sinks into it. "One of the games I was good at was a strategy game, where you could build relationships with your neighbours, or go to war. The warmongers always ended up worse off than the players who chose diplomacy."

"In a game?" Otho frowns. "So what?"

"The software was developed by political scientists, who uploaded every real-world event from history into the system's intelligence. Before the food wars, it was used to make political decisions. Afterward, its creators had the bright idea to turn the software into a game and make money from it."

Otho fixes me with a glare. "If you don't want war, why send your knights here to burn our grain stores?"

"It was a mistake. I apologize." I shift on my hard, uncomfortable chair. "Even if you decide not to trade with us, I'll ship you enough food so your people won't go hungry."

"And if I agree to negotiate a peace treaty? What do you want from me?"

"I'd like you to sell some of your produce to Triton on an ongoing basis. That's all. And we'll make sure the arrangement doesn't leave you with any shortages."

Otho glances at Tori, and a silent conversation I can't read passes between them. Does Tori know who I really am? Cale probably told her, if they've been able to talk privately. Hopefully she's on my side and hasn't tried to convince Otho that I'm his enemy.

"Why do you want our fruits and vegetables so badly?" Otho asks.

Truth is, I'm not sure of the answer. Sentin seemed to think it would mean that one day Deiterra and Triton could unite, but knowing him, he was talking about something that might happen decades from now. And I can hardly tell the prince that I'm striking this deal because I made a promise to the man who killed his father.

"We don't have any food like yours," I say instead. "Tritoners will be eager to taste it."

As soon as the words are out of my mouth, I can't help but think how weak that reasoning sounds. But to my surprise, Otho nods as though I've given him the answer he was expecting.

"High demand, high profits." He arches his eyebrows. "No doubt you'll make a fortune."

"That's the idea." I smile and lean back a little, pretending I'm comfortable even though this chair was clearly designed by someone who'd only ever heard about sitting and never actually done it.

"I'm no expert," says Cale. "But I think with the right technology, you could easily double or triple your farming output. There's no reason you can't grow enough food and vegetables to feed all your people, and export to Triton as well."

Otho looks up at the ceiling, clearly thinking over the possibilities. After a moment, his gaze comes back to me and his expression hardens. "There's something else we need to discuss. You can manufacture more Knight Skins in your factories. How do I know you won't go back to Triton and build another Skin army to invade us?"

"You have my word."

"That's not enough."

Cale leans forward, his elbows on his knees and his hands clasped together. "What if we banned Skins altogether? We could close down all development of the technology."

I frown at him, already shaking my head. There's no way I can do that. What about my beautiful Leopard Skin? The scientists have been making it better, faster, stronger, and I haven't even had the chance to try it yet.

Otho purses his lips, considering the offer in silence for several long seconds. "I'd need to send in overseers, to make sure all trace of the technology is destroyed," he says finally. "Every factory that makes them, every research center, every laboratory. No exceptions."

Cale nods. "And in return, you'd destroy the Knight Skins you have. Skins would need to be outlawed on both sides of the wall."

Otho's gaze turns to me. With an effort, I make my expression as neutral as I can.

"I'll think about it," I say.

His eyes narrow. "Ban all Skins. Permanently. Or there's no deal."

My gaze drags slowly to Cale. He's the only one who understands how it'll feel to give up my Leopard Skin. *Again.*

"We're better off without Skins." Cale drops his voice, speaking just to me as though we're alone. "The technology is too dangerous. We've seen what it can do in the wrong hands."

Otho frowns, probably wondering what he's talking about.

My heart feels like it's breaking. Nobody knows about President Morelle's Skin, so at least I'll get to keep using it. But I can't stand the thought of my Leopard Skin being destroyed.

Still, I manage to nod. "I'll disband the Skin program."

"And destroy all the Skins?" he insists.

I nod again, unable to say it aloud.

"Good." Otho leans back. "My coronation is on Friday. I'm willing to accept the deal in principle. We can hammer out the details, and finalize it once I've been crowned."

It's only Tuesday. I can't bear to spend another three days shut up in the palace, regretting ever coming here, and worrying about what the Beast might be doing in Triton.

"I have official duties in Triton, and I've been away for too long. You understand how many demands there are on a leader, don't you? I need to get home."

Otho frowns, his gaze flicking quickly to Tori. "You want to leave right away?"

"Duty calls." I give him an apologetic look. "But if Tori wouldn't mind staying behind, she could make sure the lines of communication stay open between us. In fact, the first thing we should do is set up an open channel so we can talk. I want closer ties between Deiterra and Triton. We've been separated for too long."

Tori shrugs. "I could stay for a while," she says in a voice that's a little too casual.

Otho's frown smooths away. "It'd be helpful to have you here."

I don't think they're a couple yet, but judging from the way the prince is looking at her, he's smitten. Tori's been through a lot, and I'm not sure she'll be ready to open up to anyone so soon after Gareth's death, but I hope she gives him a chance. She deserves to be happy.

I stand up, relieved to prise myself out of the uncomfortable chair, and cross to Otho to offer an outstretched hand. "Let's seal our agreement, in principle at least. We'll start by delivering a shipment of food to you as a sign of good faith, and go from there."

Otho stands up and puts his hand in mine. His handshake is firm. "Very well. I'll look forward to trading with you."

"We can also send a delegation of scientists and engineers to help with reviving your infrastructure," suggests Cale.

The prince offers his hand to Cale and the two men shake.

"What was the name of that game you played?" asks Otho.

"*Utopia.*"

Otho's mouth twitches. "Utopia," he repeats. "Let's hope so."

"We'll make it so," I tell him.

I've fulfilled my promise to Sentin, and everything he wanted is coming to pass. I only wish he were here to see it.

SIXTEEN

Otho has his driver take Cale and me as close as we can get to the wall. His imperators escort us the rest of the way, but the walk back to Triton seems longer and slower than when we walked in the other direction. It feels like forever until we've made it through the gap in the wall, picking our way through the rubble until the two of us are finally back in Triton.

The stompers guarding the wall stand to attention when they see us, and I give them a nod.

"We're finally home," I say to Cale, hearing the relief in my voice.

"You missed Triton?" he asks.

"Being shut in a room wasn't much fun. Especially with legionnaires always at my door."

"I didn't like living in the palace either. It reminded me of Morelle spying on us while we were training for the Skin Hunter contest."

I glance back at the stompers, then look ahead to the gloomy streets of Old Triton. I can already make out a group of rough sleepers camped out in an alley, far enough from the breach for the stompers not to bother them.

"Compared to Old Triton, Deiterra should have been paradise. I can't believe I'm so happy to see dark, crowded streets."

Cale taps his band as he walks. "At least we can finally get back on the network. Change your settings and you should be able to connect." He punches the change into his control panel, then stops so abruptly I almost walk into him. "Something bad must have happened while we were away. I have dozens of missed calls and messages."

I pull up my own band's control panel. As soon as I connect, message alerts start appearing. My chest gets tight when I see how many there are.

Cale is already reading his messages, and his expression is growing darker.

"There've been riots." His jaw clenches. "Your food factories were bombed. Food production had to stop, and now there are shortages."

"Bombed?" Anger rises in my gut. "Was it the Beast?"

"Who else?" His eyes are dark with rage. "Now he's selling his own food at inflated prices, and some Old Tritoners can't afford to eat."

One of the alerts on my band catches my attention. "I have a message from him. And it's a long one."

"From the Beast?"

Instead of answering, I start the recording. The Beast's face projects above my band, and I turn the sound setting to broadcast so Cale can hear what he says.

"Hello, President Morelle." The Beast pauses, grinning in a smug way that sets my teeth on edge. "Or whomever you really are inside that Skin. I heard you went away, travelling across the other side of the wall, and you lost all your knights. What a terrible shame."

I meet Cale's shocked gaze. "How does he know about the knights?"

Cale shakes his head. "Maybe the same way Sentin was communicating with Detierra. He must have a contact over there to feed him information."

The possibility raises a lot of questions, but I can't dwell on what it means, because the Beast is speaking again.

"I decided to look for your real body," he says. "Your human body. I want to know exactly who it is I'm dealing with." The image changes, the camera zooming back to take in more of the Beast's surroundings. He's standing in a room. When I recognise it, my heart spasms as though my chest has been hit with an electric shock. Behind him, a large window gives an incredible view of both New Triton and Deiterra. It's the only place in Triton where you can see right over the wall.

"It wasn't difficult to get past your security, and to the top of your building." The Beast gazes around my living room in my penthouse apartment. "You really should have your security system updated."

"Shit," breathes Cale.

I can't say a word. My throat is so dry it's feels like it's sealed shut.

"I was certain I'd find your human body in your apartment. I thought, where else would you leave it?" The Beast frowns into the camera. "Only it isn't here, is it? Clever you, hiding it somewhere else."

"He didn't find the hidden room," murmurs Cale. "And he can't have found your body, or he would have wiped your chip by now."

"You aren't here," says the Beast. "But someone else is."

My entire body goes cold even before Felicity's terrified face appears in the holo image.

"Go away," demands Felicity, her voice shaking. "Go away!"

"But don't you want to play a game?" The Beast widens his eyes as though he's trying to look innocent.

Felicity shrinks backward. "I don't want to."

"Oh, but you'll want to play when you see how much fun we can have." He claps one giant, meaty hand around her wrist. She tries to yank away, crying and struggling to get free, but I know how strong the Beast is. She doesn't stand a chance.

He drags her closer to the living room's big feature window. "Don't blame me for this," he tells her. "You know who's really to blame? The person using President Morelle's Skin. The person who decided to take a trip out there." He points to the green fields of Deiterra with his free hand. "Instead of staying here to make sure nothing bad happens to you."

"I don't want to play with you." Tears run down Felicity's cheeks.

"Do you know who's using President Morelle's Skin?"

Felicity shakes her head, letting out loud, gulping sobs. "I don't know."

"They didn't tell you anything, did they? They just left you here all alone."

"Let me go," she wails. "Let me go."

"I will let you go," he soothes. "But first, let's get some fresh air." He kicks the window, slamming one foot into it so hard it shakes.

Thanks to the new, extra-thick glass Sentin installed, it doesn't break. A rush of air escapes my lips. It's not relief. No, it can't be called relief, because Felicity is still in terrible danger. But for an awful moment I thought he was going to smash the glass and throw her out.

"What the hell?" he snarls. "You think some toughened glass is going to stop me?"

The Beast lets Felicity go so he can snatch a gun from under his coat. He fires at the window, squeezing the trigger over and over again. Felicity curls into a ball on the floor with her hands over her ears. Gunshots ring out, and small, dark circles appear in the glass, but it doesn't break.

The Beast pulls an ammunition clip out of his pocket and reloads. Then he empties the gun into the glass, making a tight circle of marks.

When it still doesn't break, the Beast kicks inside the damaged circle of glass, grunting with effort as he throws his immense weight against it. The glass shudders and shakes. Cracks appear, snaking all the way up to the window frame. With one last kick, the glass shatters. The Beast grabs what's left of the pane and yanks it roughly out of the frame.

Felicity moans, curling up even tighter as wind howls in through the broken window.

Cale makes a choking sound.

My body is as tight as a clenched fist. Every muscle strains, and my heart is hammering so hard it hurts. All I want is to reach into the holo image and pull Felicity to safety.

Instead, the Beast is the one who reaches for her. He bends to take hold of her arms, then drags her up to her feet.

"Don't," whispers Cale. "You can't do that. Let her go." I don't think he knows he's speaking the words aloud.

"It's time to play our game now." The Beast gives Felicity a horrible, leering smile. "We're going to see if you can fly."

"No," whispers Cale. "No, no, no."

My eyes are burning and prickling. There's a hard knot in my throat that feels like it's made of both fire and tears. Like all my rage and grief and denial has been compressed into a tight ball that's too hot to swallow.

"Don't." Felicity's sobbing so hard she can barely get the word out. "I don't want to play."

"Shhh," says the Beast. "What if you find out you can fly? Wouldn't that be fun? Wouldn't that be the best game ever?"

"I don't want to. Don't make me."

He pushes her into the space where the glass used to be, holding her in the rushing wind. The camera angle changes to show the impossible drop below her, the distant ground that's one hundred and ninety-seven floors away. The bastard doesn't want us to miss a thing.

Felicity is too scared even to scream. She's hanging onto his hands, trying to scramble back inside. Only strangled gasps come from her mouth, as though she's fighting desperately to catch her breath.

"This isn't my fault." The Beast stares into the camera. "I'm not the one who decided to change a perfectly good system, and bleed respectable businessmen dry. I'm not the one who decided to give everything away to a bunch of dirty sewer rats, and upset Triton's peace and prosperity." He shakes his head, his lips pressed together. "You know who's to blame, don't you, Felicity? You have one chance to save yourself. Tell me who's using the Skin, and I'll leave you unharmed."

"She doesn't know anything," whispers Cale.

I'd give anything to be able to close my eyes and not have to watch what's going to happen. Felicity can't tell the Beast what he wants to know. I doubt she even understands the question. Her eyes are wild, and she's staring down at the ground far below, struggling against his iron grip, trying to pull herself back inside.

"You're not going to tell me?" The Beast heaves a giant sigh.

Then he shoves her.

Felicity windmills her arms, trying to regain her balance even as she plummets from the window. The camera follows her down, but now, finally, I can drag my eyes away.

I fumble for the control panel and shut the recording off, before leaning over to retch up my guts.

No doubt the Beast focused the camera back on himself after Felicity hit the ground. He probably delivered some last pithy threat, telling me he's going to do the same thing to my human body. If he did, it doesn't matter. I don't need to hear it from a recording. Whatever he has to say to me, he can say in person.

It's likely he's set some kind of trap for me. Killing Felicity was probably his way to lure me to him. I don't care. I'm going to find him anyway.

He's going to pay for what he's done.

SEVENTEEN

Felicity's gone.

Cale and I stand in the living room of the apartment, staring at the broken window. It's starting to rain, and fat drops are landing inside. The floor's getting soaked.

I think we were both desperately hoping the recording was some kind of trick, that Felicity wasn't really dead, and the Beast had faked the footage for some reason. Maybe to lure us here. I would have been glad to walk into a trap if it meant Felicity was still alive.

But Felicity isn't here. Wind is howling in through the broken window, just like it did in the recording. Moisture is swirling in with it, like the world is crying.

The world *should* be crying. Felicity was innocent. She lived a lonely life, shut up here so a tyrant could take her place, and she had a terrible death. I should have done more for her.

It wasn't so long ago that I stood in front of this window looking out at Triton and Deiterra and convinced myself I could change the world for the better. But my ambition has cost the lives of people I care about. And now, instead of staring out at Deiterra with big dreams and wild ideas, I'm watching the floor get ruined.

It's time to put a stop to all this. To end everything.

I tap my band to bring up the control panel and connect to my assistant. "Send somebody up to fix the broken window in the penthouse," I tell her.

"Yes, Madam President. I'll make sure they use the special impact-resistant glass that Sentin—"

"No need. Not anymore. They can just use regular glass." Now Felicity's gone, there's only one secret still hiding up here. One secret, lying in Edward Morelle's pod, in the hidden room that the Beast couldn't find. That secret will be gone soon too, when I transfer back into my human body for good.

Soon there'll be no more Skins, and no need for me to pretend to be President Morelle. Someone else can be President of Triton. I don't want the job anymore. All I need now is revenge.

Cale turns to me, his face lined with grief. "What are you going to do?"

"I'm going to kill the Beast." Amazingly, it comes out sounding calm and perfectly reasonable.

I walk away from the window, heading toward the kitchen. I can't stand to see the broken window, or the view toward Deiterra anymore. Better to be in the enclosed space of the kitchen with its cold white stools and gleaming bench tops.

Cale follows me. "I'm going to help you," he says. "But we need a plan. The Beast blew up your factories and killed Felicity to make you angry. He wants you to go charging into his building to confront him, which means he's planning to ambush you."

"It's not an ambush if I know he's waiting for me."

"He thinks he can beat you." Cale leans against the kitchen counter, his arms folded. "And maybe he's right. We have no idea how strong his Skin is. If he's not afraid of you, he could be stronger than you are."

"He expects me to go and see him in this Skin. But I'm going in my Leopard Skin, and I doubt he knows my scientists have been busy upgrading it."

"They have?" His eyes glint. "I don't suppose they upgraded my Tiger Skin while they were at it?"

"I don't think so. Sorry. But you should use it anyway."

"Shame we don't have any knights to take with us."

"No knights," I agree. "But we have the Wasp Skin and the Devil Bear Skin." I don't mention Sentin's Reptile Skin. I'm not sure I could bear to see anyone else use it.

"Who can we ask to use those Skins? Keren and Spade?"

"I wish it were that easy. Remember how long we trained for the contest, learning to use them?" I meet his gaze, watching his puzzlement turn to shocked realization.

"You can't ask Brugan and Aza to help us."

"Why not?"

"Because Brugan's an asshole. And there's the small matter of how much he hates you."

"He hates Milla, not President Morelle. She'll be the one asking for a favor, and I bet both Brugan and Aza will jump at a chance to use their Skins one more time."

Cale blinks a few times, digesting this suggestion. "What will you tell them?"

"The truth. The Beast is using an illegal humanoid Skin and I need their help to take him down. I'm not asking them to kill a real person, just disable a Skin. We spent weeks training to do exactly that in the Skin Hunter contest, so they shouldn't find it too hard."

"But if you're using your Leopard Skin, Brugan will know who you are. What's to stop him turning on you?"

I lift my chin. "If he tries, he'll regret it."

He blows out his breath and nods. "You're right, I suppose he will. I thought you were fearless when I met you, but now? Brugan had better watch out."

I'd expected Cale to try to talk me into playing it safe and not taking risks. This is better. He finally accepts that I can take care of myself, and it makes me glad.

"Where do you think the Beast's real body will be stored?" I ask. "In the Phoenix Industries building?"

"It seems likely. But we should do some research." Cale taps his band. "You search b-Net and I'll search Sub Zero. Cross reference any mentions of the Beast with property he owns, and we'll narrow it down from there."

I do what he asks, scrolling through information until my head is spinning. "According to b-Net, he owns five factories in Old Triton and two buildings in New Triton," I tell Cale. "But it doesn't make sense for him to store his body in them. They're all busy operations, with plenty of staff and nowhere to hide a pod."

"That's weird." Cale frowns at his band's holo screen. "I found something." He enlarges the view so I can see the scraper he's looking at. It's a 3-D model of the Phoenix Industries building, an impressive steel-and-glass structure. On the top floor is the boardroom where I confronted the Beast.

I shake my head. "He can't be there. All the floors in the building can be publicly accessed. He doesn't own a private apartment like I do."

"There's no obvious hiding place." He raises his eyebrows. "That's the point. The New Triton part of the building is fifty-eight floors high, and underneath it is one of his Old Triton factories."

He adjusts the view, so the camera zooms down to Old Triton. Now I'm looking at a large, ugly factory with thick concrete walls. It's the base of the building that supports the rest.

"And?" I ask.

"Old Triton is twenty-eight stories high, but the Beast's factory is only twenty stories. It's not tall enough, yet it's supporting an entire skyscraper on top of it. See?"

He pulls up a blueprint of the building, positioning it over the 3-D model. The grid lines of the blueprint stop after twenty floors.

"What's inside the eight floors that aren't in the blue-prints?" I ask. "A private apartment? He doesn't need eight floors to store one pod."

"It's worth checking out, don't you think?"

I peer at the image. "There are no windows in that part of the building, and I bet you can't get up there from the factory below."

"You can probably go down in the elevator from New Triton. But if it's anything like Morelle's elevator, there'll be layers of security. Facial recognition, a retina scan, finger-prints. And we don't have Sentin to help us crack it."

At the mention of Sentin, a wave of grief hits me, and I swallow hard, fighting not to let it show on my face. I still can't believe he's gone. First him, and now Felicity. It's too much to bear.

My limbs feel weak and I sit heavily on one of the stools, resting my arms on the counter.

"You okay?" Cale sinks onto the stool next to me. I guess I wasn't so good at keeping my expression impassive.

"Fine." I drag in a breath, swallowing down my sorrow.

We have work to do and I don't have time to fall apart. "I'll find a way to get us down into that space."

He studies me for a moment, then nods. "I believe you will," he says softly.

"I'm also going to make sure the Morelle Corporation can keep going without me. The bombings have already caused chaos. My employees depend on their wages, and if something happens to me, I don't want the factories to have to shut down."

Cale's jaw tightens, but he nods. I can see on his face that he's thinking the same thing I am. If we confront the Beast and he manages to destroy my Leopard Skin, there's a chance my human body could die with it.

"What will you do with Morelle's Skin?" he asks.

"I'll lock it with my human body in the secret room behind the library shelves. Nobody will find it there."

"If you don't transfer back into that Skin, people will think the President of Triton vanished into thin air."

"You could transfer into it."

"Me?" He rocks back on his stool. "No thanks." He shakes his head firmly. "Triton can manage without an interim president until the election."

"No matter what happens, I'm giving all my factories to the Fist."

His eyes widen. "You're giving them all away?"

"The factories should belong to the Old Tritoners who work in them. The Fist will make sure the workers are looked after. And there are enough members that no one person will have total control. Hopefully, that'll keep them honest."

He thinks it through, and I can see the idea settling into him. "It'll be a huge change for Triton," he says finally.

"Workers owning their own factories? That's something I'd like to see."

"I don't know if it'll work, but it's guaranteed to make the industrialists angry. And anything they don't like is top of my list of things to do."

"Good enough for me." He stands up, shaking out his arms as though prepping for a fight. "Are you going to call Brugan and Aza anytime soon? Because I'm ready to get to the part where we kill the Beast."

"Think I should warn them it's a trap and the Beast will be waiting for us?"

He waves a dismissive hand. "They'll find out when we get there."

EIGHTEEN

The only two places I've ever used my Clouded Leopard Skin are in the Morelle scraper, and in the arena when I competed in the Skin Hunter contest.

Now Cale and I are bounding down the middle of an open New Triton road, heading toward Phoenix Industries.

My heart is thundering and rocket fuel burns through my veins. My Leopard Skin is a little more solid and slightly heavier than it used to be, but my increased strength more than makes up for it. Running in this Skin is still the best feeling in the world.

My paws eat up the ground in giant strides that feel like flying. Cale and I are both running fast enough to only catch brief glimpses of the shocked faces of the pedestrians we run past. Fast enough that we dodge around cabs as though they're standing still. In my upgraded and improved Skin, I'm faster than I ever could have imagined. But as hard as it is not to let myself stretch out, I restrict myself to the speed of Cale's Sabre-toothed Tiger Skin, forcing myself not to outpace him.

I glance back to see Aza and Brugan a little way behind

us. When I spoke to them as President Morelle, they were enthusiastic about the chance to use their Skins again. Since then, I've been keeping clear to avoid wasting time with a confrontation. But I imagine they're enjoying this as much as I am.

Aza's black-and-red Wasp Skin is faster than Brugan's, with her wings helping to lift her up and propel her forward with every long stride. Brugan's lumbering at her heels, his Skin big and heavy in contrast to her slender frame. His wolfish face is as sinister as ever, and his fur-covered Devil Bear Skin shakes the ground with every stride.

The Phoenix Industry scraper is just ahead. Beside me, Cale runs with his mouth open and his tongue lolling between his elongated top fangs. His eyes are alight with such a fierce joy, it makes me want to laugh with delight.

When we reach the base of the scraper, we both leap at once, hooking our claws into the edge of the large Phoenix Industries sign above the front doors. The building is coated in textured concrete, and our razor-sharp claws cut into its surface, so climbing the outside of the tower is almost too easy. We haul ourselves up it as quickly as we used to go up the never-wall.

Near the top of the building, the giant phoenix logo is made from polished steel. It juts out from the concrete, and I pause for a moment, balanced on its curve. The board-room window is just above it, so we can lever off it to crash our way in.

The other two are below us, and I want to keep ahead of them so they can follow our lead.

"You ready for anything?" I ask Cale. "The Beast will have seen us coming."

Cale's lips peel back in a snarl. "Ready."

"Let me go first—"

But Cale's already throwing himself at the window, claws outstretched to crash through. I follow so closely behind him that shards of glass are still hitting the floor as I land.

The Beast stands in front of us. He has an enormous gun levelled at us.

He's cleared this entire floor of furniture, to make it an open, empty space. Behind him are five giant, hairy animals. They're standing upright, but their chests are as round as barrels, and their arms are bulging with muscles and so long, they hang to their knees. They're enormous apes, but with their upper bodies so grotesquely oversized, they look like cartoons. Like the gorilla from the retro version of *Donkey Kong*.

I have a feeling Morelle's scientists didn't make these Skins. Not when they were so meticulous about not changing the appearance of my leopard. I bet the Beast manufactured them himself.

"Two against six," gloats one of the ape men. "You're outnumbered and outgunned."

I recognise his voice. It's one of the businessmen who were with the Beast when I barged into his boardroom. If the apes are all businessmen and not used to fighting, at least we'll have an advantage.

Aza and Brugan hurtle through the window and land on the floor behind us. Brugan snarls when he sees the Skins. Aza unfurls her red wings and extends the stingers from her palms.

We're still outnumbered, but we'll put up a damn good fight.

The Beast hitches his giant weapon further onto his shoulder, pointing it at me. The stench of its fuel is sharp and strong, burning the back of my throat.

Before the Beast can squeeze the trigger, I leap for his throat.

Cale jumps at the same time, and both of us arc toward the Beast. Flames shoot from his weapon, unbearable heat blasting into my face. Instantly I remember the feeling of super-heated polymer spurting from a machine at the factory, searing my flesh away and burning out my eye. I twist in mid-air and fall to the side, panic filling me, so all I can think of is getting away. The stench of burning hair and flesh fills my throat and lungs.

The Beast sweeps his weapon toward me, but I'm already leaping again. I slam into one of the ape creatures, bowling it over. Desperate to escape the flames, I claw at the creature. I gouge chunks from its hairy body, my claws lacerating its over-muscled arms and chest. It howls in pain as I rip flesh from bone.

The flames die, and for a moment I can't hear anything but my own racing heartbeat, or see anything but white spots still burning in front of my eyes. Then my vision clears.

Beside me, Aza is fighting one of the apes, slashing it with her stingers. Her movements are as graceful as a dance, so precise and beautiful that watching her fight clears the panic from my brain.

My fur is singed, but I'm not hurt. The flame thrower is on the floor, still smoking, either abandoned or knocked out of the Beast's hands by Brugan, who's wrestling with him.

Cale was just as much in the flamethrower's blast as I was. Where is he?

An ape charges at me. Adrenaline's pumping through my muscles, and I rear up to swipe the ape to the side, sending it tumbling. The Beast slams Brugan against the ground, and an ape leaps on the fallen devil bear. Brugan and the ape are both giants, equal in size, and Brugan curses at the top of his lungs as he struggles to throw the creature off.

I move to help him, digging my claws into the ape and hauling it off Brugan so he can scramble to his feet. Behind them, I finally see Cale. He rears up over the Beast, plunging down with his claws. But the Beast grabs him by the forelegs and slams him against the wall.

Snarling, Brugan tackles the ape again. I throw myself at the Beast's back. One of my claws digs into his shoulder, gouging a wound deep enough that a human would go down screaming. He barely seems to notice.

One of the ape creatures grabs me from behind, latching onto my front leg with giant hands. Snarling, I manage to sink my teeth into its shoulder. With a mighty jerk of my jaws, I tear a mouthful of flesh away.

The creature roars, stumbling back, as I spit blood at it. Its arm hangs uselessly. Another creature is on me at once, but I slash it with my claws, ripping its flesh to shreds.

Cale circles the Beast, feinting forward and back as he looks for an opening. He's limping, holding his front paw off the ground. His legs are stained red, his fur clumped with so much blood that it spatters onto the floor with every movement. As he turns away from me, I see the burn that covers one side of his body. His beautiful fur has been seared away and his flesh is raw.

Yanking my claws out of the ape creature, I rush to help him. The Beast tugs a long knife from under his shirt and brandishes it at me. I leap at him anyway, remembering what the scientist said about having a protective shield in my flesh.

He stabs me, mid-leap. Pain sears through my chest, but the knife only digs in a little way. Surprise flashes in the

Beast's eyes when it won't penetrate. I slam into him as I land, sending him sprawling backward. Then I claw at his knife arm, slicing through his clothing and into his flesh as easily as I cut through the apes. The upgrades to my Leopard Skin have made me stronger than any of them.

With a roar of pain and rage, the Beast tears away.

I go after him, slashing big cuts across his back, and turning his shirt to ribbons soaked with his blood. He turns and slams his fist into my side, a powerhouse punch that bowls me sideways.

I hit an ape, knocking it over. It grabs me as it falls, pulling me with it so I land on top of it. Its hands wrap around my throat, cutting off my air. Before I can wrench free, Aza looms over us. She stabs downward, thrusting her stinger through its eye. Its grip loosens and I push away from it, pulling myself back onto four paws. The floor is slippery with blood, and my front paws slide forward so I almost go down again.

Chest heaving, I look around.

The Beast has his knife in his hand, and his knees bent in a fighting stance. He snarls, facing off against Brugan. Both are badly wounded, their arms and torsos slashed with cuts, The Beast's shirt is torn away, and there barely seems like enough flesh left to hold his guts in.

Aza circles around to get behind him. Her wings are tattered and useless, and her black armor has been torn away from her body in several places. The flesh underneath is raw and bloody.

Littered around the room, the apes are mostly still. The businessmen must have transferred back into their own human bodies. All except two, who are struggling to rise, but too badly injured to be much of a threat.

Cale is on the floor, his legs sprawled out. His breath is

loud, and my chest hurts to see him so badly wounded. Before I can go to him, I need to finish the Beast. Though Brugan and Aza are challenging him, compared to them, I'm barely injured. I leap over a dead ape, landing in front of them.

"I've got this," I say with a growl.

"Come on." The Beast brandishes his knife at me. "Come and get me."

I launch myself forward, claws outstretched. He slashes at me, but his knife hits one of my claws and goes flying. I land on his chest, bowling him over.

As he struggles to rise, I hear Tori's voice in my head. *Don't give him a chance to catch his balance. Only losers play fair.*

I thrust my claws into his neck.

He gurgles, blood dribbling from his mouth. His glare is full of hatred. His mouth opens as though he's going to say something, then his eyes go blank, and he slumps. He must have transferred his consciousness back into his human body.

Pulling my claws from his throat, I pad over to touch my nose to Cale's. "Are you okay?"

His beautiful Tiger Skin stinks of burnt flesh, a stench that turns my stomach. His long saber-teeth are red with blood and his golden eyes are dull with pain. Still, he manages to lift his head. "I'm okay," he lies.

Aza curses. Her black wasp's helmet doesn't show any emotion, but her voice is full of anger. "President Morelle told us we'd be fighting one humanoid Skin. Not these hideous creatures." She kicks one of the apes.

Brugan gives her a gruesome smile, peeling his lips away from his bloody fangs. "I liked killing them." He scans the room as though hoping more will appear.

"Thanks for killing the ape that had me by the neck," I say to Aza.

"You killed most of them." She runs her hand over the torn armor on her torso and sucks in air. "And yet you're barely injured. Why not?"

"Yeah, how'd your Skin get so strong?" Brugan snarls. "The flames didn't burn you."

Aza spreads what's left of her wings. "Something's going on that you're not telling us. I want to know what it is."

I shoot Cale a glance. "My Skin was upgraded. Because, ah, I've been working with President Morelle, helping her track down people who're making illegal Skins."

Brugan takes a step toward me, and his voice drops dangerously low. "That's a lie. She'd never choose a sewer rat to help her."

He probably expects me to back down. Instead, I flick my tail from side to side, snarling up into his wolfish face.

"I may not have won the contest," I growl. "But I lasted longer than you did. And now my Skin is stronger, faster, and better than yours will ever be."

He lifts his claws. "Oh yeah? Then it's time for a rematch, little kitty cat. Come here, and I'll carve you into kitty shreds."

It's such an empty threat that my flash of anger fades away and I sit back on my haunches. He's all hot air and bluster. Was I ever afraid of him? The idea seems laughable.

"That's enough, Brugan." Cale pulls himself up onto all four paws. He stands with his head and tail lowered, but his hackles are up. "We still have work to do and I won't let you—"

"I'm leaving." Aza cuts him off, turning toward the stairwell. "You might not care about your Skins, but mine needs urgent repair." Torn pieces of her ruined wings drag on the floor as she stalks away.

"Wait," I say to her back. "Please help me get Cale to the lobby. They'll need to send a car to pick him up—"

Cale turns his face to me. "I'm not leaving. I'm staying with you."

"You're too badly hurt."

"A few scratches, that's all."

Aza pauses to glance over her shoulder. She waves one of her hands, graceful even when she's being dismissive. "Cale's fine. And I've done everything President Morelle asked. Now I intend to ask for the same modifications she gave your Skin."

Brugan stares after her, clearly not wanting to let her get away. He aims one more snarl in my direction. "Next time you won't get off so lightly, sewer rat." Then he hurries after Aza.

Cale starts to groan, but manages to muffle it, turning it into a loud exhale. Blood still drips from his fur, but his eyes are fiercely determined.

"I won't leave you, so don't ask me again." His firm tone makes it a command.

I stretch my muzzle to his. He smells like burned fur and pain, but underneath is a will forged in iron.

"Then let's go," I say.

NINETEEN

The elevators to go down to the lobby are at the other end of this floor. If Cale weren't so badly hurt, I'd use the stairwell like Brugan and Aza did. Instead, I smack one paw against the button to call the elevator to this level.

Cale and I cram into it when it arrives. We're two massive, feline Skins covered with blood, squeezing ourselves into an opulent, gold-and-marble carriage. The doors shut, and the elevator goes smoothly down. It's mirrored so we can stare at our own reflections while our gore drips onto its polished marble floor.

It feels like a dream. A surreal moment of unreality.

The elevator doors open on the lobby level of the building. Several office workers are waiting for the elevator. Their mouths drop open when they see us, and after a shocked second, they run.

As Cale limps out of the elevator, I turn my attention to its controls. There's no obvious button or switch to make it go down to the secret floors below.

"What now?" he asks.

In answer, I stab my front claws down into the elevator's

marble floor, shattering the marble. Raking it up, I expose a thick metal plate.

Before the scientists enhanced it, my Skin could never have punched through metal. But when I put all my strength into a downward thrust, my claws go through it and I can peel it back like ripping apart a tin can.

Behind me, Cale grunts. "Who do I see about putting in for one of those upgrades?"

With a final, mighty heave, I tear the entire metal floor out. Peering into the gloom below, I can see the elevator shaft goes down one more level. At the bottom of the shaft, a door is set into the wall. I turn to Cale. "So much for the Beast's fancy security system."

Cale flicks his tail from side to side. "Poor fool didn't think to make it leopard proof."

I'm poised to jump into the shaft when it occurs to me that Cale may not be able to follow. His breathing is still too fast and it's obvious he's in a lot of pain. "Will you be able to get down there?" I ask.

"I'll manage."

"You could stay here and—"

"I'll manage," he growls.

I hesitate a moment longer, then drop into the hole, landing softly on the bottom of the shaft. Cale lands heavily behind me with a grunt of pain that he doesn't manage to swallow. Together, we step out into the first of the Beast's hidden levels.

It's a huge, bustling space, filled with glass-fronted offices that back onto the outer walls. In the middle of the floor is a central, open well, and looking down into it, I see four more floors. A circular staircase provides access to them, solving the mystery as to why the elevator shaft only went down one floor.

The lights are bright in here, and the atrium in the center of the building gives it a sense of openness, in spite of not having any windows.

People dressed in white lab coats are gaping at us. In the glass-walled rooms, more white-coated people are working.

They're laboratories. Just like in the Morelle scraper and in Deiterra, the Beast's scientists are working on Skins.

Ignoring the gaping scientists, Cale limps slowly toward the central atrium. I pad along with him, peering into the labs we pass. Like they were at the Morelle Corportation, the scientists are experimenting on dissected brains and body parts.

"No wonder the Beast has hidden his research department away," says Cale. "This work is illegal. Skin research is supposed to be regulated." He's limping slowly, like every muscle hurts. I stick close to him, ready to support him if he can't stay upright.

"Why can we only see five floors?" He flicks his ears toward the atrium where the other levels are visible. "According to the blueprints, there should be eight."

"Let's find somebody to ask."

As we walk down the open, circular staircase to the next floor, we get a good view into all the labs we pass. Some of the experiments are stomach-churning, although I saw similar things in the Morelle scraper.

Word quickly spreads that two large Skins are moving through the department, and some of the scientists decide it's time to leave, heading toward the elevators with worried expressions. I watch them closely, looking for the right person to interrogate. Someone with an air of authority about them.

I spot a couple of likely-looking scientists in one of the

labs, and plant myself in front of them, doing my best to loom over them menacingly.

"Been working here long?" I growl.

One of the women has allowed some fine wrinkles to develop around her mouth and eyes. The other looks younger, though she could just be more thoroughly tweaked. but I have a feeling both are senior scientists. Neither of them cower, and they don't smell like fear. In fact, they peer at me curiously, as though fascinated by my Skin.

"I'm Doctor Moss and this is Doctor Sinjay," says the wrinkled woman, frowning at the cuts on my shoulder. "Would you mind if I take a closer look at the composition of the subcutaneous tissue—?"

"Where's the Beast's human body?"

The two scientists glance at each other, nervousness finally flickering across their expressions. "Not here," says the younger one.

"Then where?"

Doctor Moss shakes her head. "I have no idea." Though her tone is brisk, it's obvious she's lying.

"You know how to get to the hidden floors?" I ask.

"Hidden floors?" She opens her eyes too wide, and purses her mouth in a perplexed expression. She's a terrible liar.

"Why don't you show us around?" I snarl and feint toward them, so they back away. Then I herd them the way I want them to go, directing them down the stairs.

Doctor Moss keeps glancing back at Cale, who's limping beside me with glassy eyes. "You should let us take a look at that Skin," she says. "Wounds that serious are susceptible to bacterial infection. If enough tissue is corrupted, it may be beyond repair."

I glance sideways at Cale, hating the thought of his Tiger Skin dying that way.

Cale lifts his head but doesn't meet my gaze. "Just keep going." His voice is strained.

"When we get to the bottom floor, you'll need to remember how to get a little further," I tell Doctor Moss.

On the fifth level, we come to a locked door, and I motion to the band reader beside it. "Unlock it," I order the two scientists.

They both shake their heads, their eyes wide with fear. "We don't have access—" starts Doctor Moss.

"Prove it. Swipe your band."

"But it's a secure area, and strictly off limits."

Cale leans against the wall. His head is hanging down, and his sides heave. He's obviously hurting badly, and I don't know how much longer he can stay on his paws.

"Swipe it. Now." I lift one paw, extending my claws to her throat.

Doctor Moss swallows hard and holds her band to the reader. The door opens with a click.

Gunfire blasts out from behind the door. I leap sideways to shove both women to the ground. Too late. Doctor Sinjay cries out with pain, and blood soaks her white coat at the waist.

Leaving them both on the floor, I charge through the door.

Five businessmen fire at me from behind the pods they used when they transferred their consciousness into the ape creatures. The shots are deafening. Bullets slam into me, searing through my flesh and knocking me backward.

I force myself to keep struggling forward anyway, bounding toward the businessmen. The one in front of me fires at point blank range, and the bullet gazes across my forehead. For a moment I'm deaf and blind, the top of my head on fire with agony. A sharp chemical stench fills my throat, then I choke on smoke. Blood runs into my eyes.

Lashing out, I strike flesh. My ears are ringing, but I catch the clatter of a gun hitting the floor.

Dropping my head, I swipe at my eyes with one paw, trying to wipe away the blood. The room comes back into blurry focus. Instantly, I launch myself at the next man. From the corner of my eye, I see Cale push a third man to the ground.

The last two businessmen fall just as fast, and I try not to injure them too badly as I disable them. I don't want them dead. Not yet, anyway.

As painful as the gunshots were, they don't seem to have done any major damage to my Skin. I'm bleeding, but only from surface wounds. The men's guns are on the floor, and I swipe them into the hallway.

"I know who these men are," pants Cale, swaying over the man he knocked to the ground. "Big shots. Billionaires. They were the ones using the Ape Skins?" He presses his long fangs against the man's neck.

The man moans with fear. "Please, don't kill me."

"Big shots? They're criminals." I force another man onto the ground, holding him easily with one paw. When I first met these men in the Beast's boardroom, they were contemptuous and arrogant. Now, they're pale and afraid. The one who landed a shot in my forehead is the most badly hurt, with his shirt in tatters and deep lacerations in his shoulder. He's on the floor sucking in loud gasping breaths. He must be in shock, but I think he'll live. Now I have the time to look at his face, I see he's the man the Beast called Harrison.

"I'll give you anything," says the man under my paw. "Tell me what you want and it's yours."

"I want the Beast."

"If I show you where he is, will you let me go?"

"I'll show you," another of the men volunteers quickly. "I never wanted to attack President Morelle. I advised against it, but the Beast didn't listen. Let me show you where he is."

I glance at Cale as he staggers sideways and sits heavily. To add to all his other injuries, I think he's been shot. His fur is a mess, so soaked with blood that I can't see all his wounds. His eyes are dull and his breaths rasp in and out with a faint gurgling as though he has blood in his lungs. We need to get his Skin repaired before it's beyond saving.

"What's your name?" I ask the volunteer.

"Piero. I'm the largest clothing manufacturer in Triton." He seems a little offended I didn't already know that, but all the men look so alike, they could be brothers.

I let him lead us out of the room. Doctor Sinjay is on the floor in the hallway. Doctor Moss has both hands pressed over her gunshot wound, but blood is slowly leaking around her palms.

"Come here," I order one of the businessmen. "Put pressure on her wound."

The man obeys, taking Doctor Moss's place.

"If you stop pressing on her wound, or if she dies, I'll come back and kill you," I growl at him. Then I turn to Doctor Moss. "Go and get help for her. Hurry."

I'd do more if I could, but we need to find the Beast while Cale's Skin can still walk. At least, I think he can still walk.

"Can you keep going?" I ask him.

"Of course. Just a scratch." Even talking sounds like it's difficult for him, but he pushes himself back up to standing.

I shut the rest of the businessmen back inside the room, lock the door, and put a claw through the band reader. Hopefully it'll hold them secure until I can decide what to do with them.

Piero, our volunteer, leads us to a wall that looks like all the others. It's not until I peer closely at it that I make out the hairline cracks where a hidden door can be opened.

"Nobody but the Beast can get in there," he says. "His security is state-of-the-art, and the Beast is the only one who can open the door. I don't know what's through there. Nobody's been in but him."

"Who is he?" I demand. "What's his real name?"

His eyes widen. "You don't know?" The way his voice cracks on the question is a giveaway. Whoever the Beast really is, Piero is afraid of being the one to tell us.

I rear up and plant my front paws on his chest, slamming his back against the wall. Bringing my muzzle close to his terrified face, I let my hot breath gust over him. "Tell me."

TWENTY

Piero is hard against the wall, and with my front paws on his chest, my full weight is pressing into him. Thanks to his colleague who shot me in the forehead, the fur on my face is clumped with blood, so I guess I don't look as pretty as I normally do.

When I growl, Piero nods quickly, his head jerking up and down, and his eyes large and frightened. Judging from the smell, the biggest clothing manufacturer in Triton might be in need of a clean pair of trousers.

"His real name is Kriston Welcon," he gasps.

My limbs feel suddenly weak. "Welcon Pharmaceuticals?"

Behind me, Cale draws in a sharp breath. "The Beast can't be the head of Welcon Pharmaceuticals. Kriston Welcon went to jail."

"He didn't." Piero's voice sounds strangled. With my weight on his chest, he must be struggling to breathe. "Edward Morelle gave him a Skin. That was the deal. It was the price he demanded. A new identity and a Skin that meant he could live forever."

"The deal?" I lean on him a little harder. "What do you mean?"

"His payment for the Welcon disaster."

"You planned it all, didn't you?" Cale's tone is blunt, but I can hear his rage simmering under the surface. "When Welcon put out his cancer vaccine, he knew what would happen. He knew it'd cause a fertility spike and millions of unplanned babies. All of you knew in advance. I'm sure Edward Morelle did."

"Did you know too?" I snarl at Piero.

The man's eyes are starting to bulge. I'm tempted to lean harder and crush him. Instead, I ease my weight a little so he can drag in a loud, gasping breath.

"I knew about it," he pants. "But it wasn't my idea."

Dropping to four paws, I pace up and down in front of the cowering man, my anger too intense to keep still. I can trace everything bad that ever happened to my family back to the Welcon disaster. It caused misery for millions. My father worked himself to death trying to pay second-child taxes. And they did it on *purpose?*

"Why?" I snarl, too furious to manage more than one word.

"It was just business," Piero says, rubbing his chest. "We had the president where we wanted him. We could make Triton better. Back then, there was only one Triton. One city for everyone, and nowhere to get away from the crowds. We needed to expand upward, and the surge in second-child taxes meant we could build New Triton." He's speaking fast, the words spilling out in a rush. "Before Welcon, there was a labor shortage. Afterward, plenty of people needed work. Our factories were at full capacity again, and in New Triton we had the room to build proper houses. We built safer communities for our families, and better—"

I swipe him hard across the face with one paw, sending him sprawling against the wall. I've never experienced fury like this. My vision has gone red, and my blood feels like it's boiling in my veins. I want to kill them all. I want to rip every one of the cruel, greedy industrialists to pieces, and make them scream their regrets.

Cale moves in front of me, putting himself between me and the cowering man. He growls, and my rage is reflected in his eyes. "Let's go and find Kriston Welcon," he snarls.

I hesitate, fighting for control. Then I manage to nod. "Go," I hiss at Peiro through clenched fangs. "Before I kill you."

He doesn't need to be told twice. He pushes himself to his feet and staggers quickly away.

Turning to the secret door, I unleash my fury by tearing into it with my claws. The door is thick and solid, but I splinter it into matchsticks.

Beyond it is a narrow stairwell going down. There are cameras in the ceiling, and at the bottom of the stairs is another metal door with a band reader next to it. The door looks thicker and heavier than the others, and it has a seal around its edge.

Too bad for the Beast, the door was built to keep humans out, not raging Leopard Skins. I slash my claws through the metal, and after gouging out the lock, I rip the whole thing out of the wall.

"Stay back," I warn Cale. "The Beast might be armed."

Stepping cautiously through the hole, I find myself in an apartment. One sweeping glance shows me the place is empty. There's a shiny, new-looking kitchen, and a luxurious living room. Instead of windows, large screens set into the walls show a picturesque view of trees and a waterfall, as if the apartment were in the middle of a forest. A bedroom is screened off in one corner, and beyond it is a bathroom.

"I think we found where the Beast sleeps," I say.

"It's more than that." Cale replies from behind me. "The seal on that door was to keep the place airtight. I bet it has its own air purifiers and clean water supply." He limps into the kitchen and swipes open a cupboard so roughly, he tears the door right off. The entire cupboard is neatly packed with food packets. "Ready for the apocalypse," he says.

"So this is what?" I ask. "A place he can hole up in case something bad happens?"

"A billionaire bolt hole." Cale limps slowly through the apartment toward a door at the far end, past the bedroom. "Can't wait to see what's on the next floor."

"Let me go first."

The next door is as thick as the last one, and sealed so it's airtight. I deal with it quickly. Beyond it is a stairwell, and at the bottom of the stairs is yet another locked, sealed door.

"So many airtight doors," growls Cale. "If someone poisoned the air outside, he would have survived. Just him and the cockroaches."

"Not anymore." Rearing onto my hind legs, I tear the door out of its frame. I'm ready to rush in and disarm the Beast, but no gunshots ring out, and I can't catch the scent of a person from inside.

I step through the damaged doorframe into a long hallway with doors coming off it on either side, and turn back to make sure Cale manages to limp through as well. We move down the hallway together, warily opening each door as we come to it. In the first room, crates are stacked from floor to ceiling. Each crate is stencilled with a list of its contents, which turn out to be meal bars. The Beast has stockpiled enough food to last for years.

The next room is full of crates holding other types of supplies, including water purifiers, medicines, gas masks, bio protection suits, and communication equipment.

In the final room we find hundreds of guns stacked in giant racks, and enough explosives to blow up all of Triton.

"Shit," breathes Cale. "Is he ready to survive an apocalypse or to start one?"

I pad down the long rows of weapons, my head spinning at how many there are. With these, the Beast could arm his own soldiers. Is that what he planned? Did he mean to create his own Skin army?

At the far end of the hallway is another door that presumably leads down to the last level. There's a good chance the Beast is past that door, in the deepest bowels of his bunker. And he's not short of munitions, so if he's rigged a booby trap, he could blow us to hell.

I turn to Cale. "Transfer back into your human body now, so you can call Spade and Keren. Tell them to come here with trucks, ready to take the Beast's supplies. All this food should go to the shelters. And I want them to take the weapons and explosives somewhere safe until I decide what to do with—"

"I told you, I'm not leaving you." His ears flatten. "You're only trying to get rid of me because the Beast must be waiting for us at the bottom of the next stairwell with some serious fire power." He flicks the tip of his tail angrily from side to side. It's probably the only uninjured part of his body. "I'm not going anywhere, Milla. You need me."

"But I'm strong enough to—"

"My Skin is expendable," he interrupts. "I'll go through the door first and if he manages to kill me, I'll transfer back to my real body. No harm done. And hopefully it'll buy you time to take him down."

"But your Tiger Skin will be destroyed."

"Skins will be illegal soon anyway. Wasn't that the deal we made with Otho?"

I drag in a breath, reluctant to let him sacrifice himself so brutally. "You love that Skin."

His eyes are dull with pain, but as he stretches his muzzle toward me, the golden flecks in their depths seem to reignite and glow with warmth. "I do. But I love you so much more. And if it comes to a choice between you or my Skin, I'll choose you every time."

My heart swells to fill my chest. I touch his nose with mine, breathing in his bloody, burned-fur scent, and tangling our whiskers together. My throat is almost too full to talk, but I manage to whisper, "I love you, too."

The words take up all the space between us. They seem too big and important for the moments before both our Skins could be torn apart. I want to say them again when we're somewhere safe, when we have all the time in the world to explore them and discover what they might mean.

Peeling my lips back from my teeth, I give him a feline grin. "Now let's go and kill the Beast."

He snorts out a small, amused breath. "It's a date."

I keep close by his side as we slowly descend the steps to the final floor, feeling every stumble and intake of breath as though his pain were mine. When we get to the last locked door, I rear up and rest my front paws on it. "You ready?" I murmur.

He meets my gaze and gives a single nod.

Plunging my claws into the door, I wrench it out of its

frame. Cale pushes past me, limping into the room before I've managed to throw the door aside.

Dropping to all four paws, I start after him.

An explosion slams into me, hurling me back into the hallway. I smash hard into the wall. Sentin's death flashes in front of my eyes, the way he blew himself up.

Cale!

A wave of heat rolls out of the splintered door frame, burning my lungs as I drag in a breath. Pulling myself up, I drop my head and lope into the searing heat.

Smoke fills the room, blinding me. The floor is hot enough to keep me moving, and I keep bounding forward, though the pads of my paws are burning.

"Cale." It's more of a cough than a word, and I already know it's useless to call for him. There's no way he could have survived the explosion.

Gunfire cracks out of the smoke, the muzzle of the Beast's gun lighting up with each shot. The bullets carve into me, but I barely feel them as I rush toward the flashes of light.

I leap over the still-burning floor where the explosion went off, and fling myself into the smoke on the other side, barrelling into the dark shape of the man behind the gunfire. Together, we slide across the floor, his weapon clattering away and hitting what remains of the large pod that was in the middle of the room, surrounded by now-shattered medical equipment.

I leap to my feet and press one paw against the man's chest before he can get up. His eyes stare up into mine. The Beast's human body looks nothing like his bald, fleshy Skin. This man looks much like all the other businessmen who sat around his boardroom table. He has thick, dark hair and a smooth, almost-ageless face. The only signs of how old he must really be are the fine lines around his tweaked eyes and mouth.

I snarl into his face. My anger is so intense, it burns hotter than the fire did.

"Stop," he croaks. "It doesn't have to be like this."

"You killed Felicity." It comes out as a growl, the words hard to make out.

"This Skin is stronger than I knew they could be." He says it accusingly, as though he's caught me cheating. "Who are you?"

"President Morelle," I growl. "Before that, I was a sinker. Expendable. Another grunt for your factories."

"An Old Tritoner?" He sounds shocked, as though this possibility never occurred to him. "But how did you—?" He gives his head a little shake. "It doesn't matter where you came from. If you're the President of Triton, you'll need me."

"I need you?" I bare my teeth, tempted to bite his arrogant head right off his shoulders.

He grunts with pain as my weight bears down on him, and turns his face to the side so he's not staring into my teeth. "Triton won't run without my consortium. It would be chaos." For the first time, there's a hint of fear in his voice.

"You organized the Welcon disaster that tore my family apart."

"I distributed the vaccine, but Edward Morelle was the mastermind behind the idea." He speaks quickly, his tone cajoling. "And if you'd just open your mind, you'd see that the aftermath of that act could give you everything you've ever wanted. Let me help you."

"I want nothing from you." I spit the words, my bloody saliva splattering his face. "You deserve to die for what you've done to millions of sinkers. Let alone what you did to Felicity."

His mouth hardens and a flash of defiance sparks in his eyes. "Then throw away everything I have to offer. But Old Triton can't survive without factories, which won't run without the consortium. Hurt me, and you'll regret it when Old Triton falls apart and your precious sewer rats are starving in the streets."

I drag in a breath, fighting for control of my rage. "I'd planned to tear your throat out. But now I have a better idea."

Lifting my paw off his chest, I flip him over. Then I slice the tip of one claw into the back of his neck, ripping out flesh. He screams, his body convulsing, but I don't stop until I've torn out the chip that allowed him to transfer into his Skin.

With the mess I've made of his flesh, I doubt he'll ever be able to implant a new one. But he won't die. He's rich enough that his blood must be filled with nanites that will keep him alive until his doctors can patch him up.

He'll be hurting for a long time though. And by the time he's healed enough to worry about the empire he's created, it'll be gone. I'm going to make sure of it.

TWENTY-ONE

Leaving Kriston Welcon bleeding on the floor, I head slowly back upstairs. The laboratory levels are now deserted, all the scientists having fled. The industrialists I locked in the room with their pods have gone too, and the door has been wrenched open.

It doesn't matter.

I move slowly, my body aching after having been burned, shot, and battered. But with every step, my sense of purpose grows. Kriston Welcon was right. New Triton depends on Old Triton, and vice versa. Without the factories to employ them, without being able to work to earn credits to buy food, Old Triton will suffer.

Unless I change everything.

I'm going to need the Fist to help me, but hopefully Cale has called Keren and Spade by now and they're on their way here. In the meantime, I start by destroying everything I can find, starting with the businessmen's pods, and moving up to the equipment in the laboratories.

I smash every computer in every lab, and grind countless experiments into the floor, turning each room into a mess of broken machinery and glass.

When I finally get to the floor with the elevators, I run into Keren and Spade. Cale must have told them I was using the Leopard Skin, but they still look nervous when they see me.

"Milla?" Keren steps closer, her unease disappearing as she hardens her jaw. It reminds me of the way she launched herself at an oncoming knight the first time I met her.

"It's me," I say.

Spade lets out a low whistle, pushing his woollen hat back from his forehead. "That's one impressive Skin. I saw it on the holo, but being this close is something else."

Keren's arm must have healed, because it's no longer strapped up. She puts out a hand to touch my shoulder, then wrinkles her nose and draws it back. "You're covered in blood."

"Only some of it's mine."

She runs her gaze over my big form. "You look pretty beaten up. Are you okay?"

"I'm tougher than I look."

Spade snorts. "You don't exactly look like a pushover. That Skin's prettier than the knights, but I still wouldn't want to get on your bad side."

"Did Cale tell you there are a lot of food supplies down here? If the Fist can transport it all out, it'll feed a lot of people." I start walking the way I've just come, leading them down to the Beast's hidden rooms. "And that's not all. There are weapons and explosives hidden away down here."

Keren frowns. "You want us to take those too?"

"There's something I need you to do with it." I slow

down, swinging my head to catch both their eyes. "I trust both of you, almost as much as I trust Cale. But there are some things I'm going to tell you that are going to be hard for you to believe. Things about Kris Welcon and Edward Morelle, and the corruption that's so much a part of Triton that it's embedded into every piece of our city. I want to change it. All of it. And to do that we need to tear it down and start again."

Spade makes a choking sound. "Don't tell me you want to blow up Triton?"

"I'll tell you what I want. But to understand why, you need to hear the whole story."

As we make our way back down to the lower floors, I tell them everything, including how Sentin killed Edward Morelle, and I became President Morelle and went to Deiterra, and that Kriston Welcon is lying injured on the bottom floor of this part of the building. Then I tell them what I plan to do next.

By the time I've finished explaining, we've reached the room with all the weapons, and Keren and Spade are gaping wide-eyed at both the racks of guns, and the plan I've laid out.

"Shit," breathes Spade softly. He rubs his bristled chin, and his grimace shows all the gaps in his teeth. "Is this for real? I mean, are you serious?"

"Deadly serious."

He shakes his head. "Don't get me wrong, I already thought you had the biggest damn balls of anyone I ever met. But shit, Milla. You've reached a boss level of bad-assery."

A light flashes on Keren's band and she brings up its control panel with glazed eyes, clearly acting on autopilot with her mind still on what I've been telling her.

Then her eyes snap back into focus and she frowns at

me. "You said President Morelle was just a Skin, right? And you were the one using it?"

"That's right."

"Then how do you explain this?"

She activates her holo display, and an image of President Morelle's face appears above it.

"What's this?" I sit back on my haunches. "A recording?

She shakes her head. "It's live. Breaking news. The president's making an announcement."

"What?" The word comes out as a shocked growl. My heart speeds up. How could this be happening? I left Morelle's Skin locked in the secret room in the private apartment, and after the Beast managed to get up there, I tripled the number of guards in the building.

How could anybody get through all that security, find the secret room, and steal the Skin?

"I'm pleased to announce a formal peace treaty has been signed with Deiterra," says President Morelle. "We now have the opportunity to trade our goods for theirs. This agreement has opened up exciting opportunities. It will have many benefits for Triton."

I swallow hard as a horrible suspicion takes root in my mind. Surely I must be mistaken about who's taken the Skin for themselves. The idea makes my stomach churn. If I'm right about this then I've been wrong about everything else. I've been betrayed.

President Morelle gazes into the camera, her expression calm and her tone firm. "To fulfil our obligations, I will immediately ban all Skins. I've asked our police force to help me enforce this ban. Effective immediately, Skin development will stop, and all existing Skins will be destroyed. Anyone using one will be arrested."

Keren and Spade both stare at me, wide-eyed, as though

a target's just appeared on my chest. Which is exactly what it feels like.

"They can make your Skin illegal, but I'd like to see them try to arrest a giant leopard," says Spade.

Keren frowns. "You should be careful. Whoever's behind this will use this as an excuse to take you down."

Lifting one paw, I motion for Keren to stop the live stream.

"My human body is in the same secret room as the President's Skin was," I tell her. "Whoever took Morelle's Skin has access to it. They can do whatever they want, including wiping my chip. That's if they don't just decide to kill me."

"What does that mean?" Keren asks.

"It means I probably don't have much time left. You need to do what I asked. Get everyone in the Fist to help. You have to do it now."

"But—"

"How quickly can you get it done?"

They exchange a troubled glance, their misgivings clear.

Spade sucks in his breath. "Are you sure this is—?"

My mind is tugged sideways, I feel dizzy, like I'm spinning. I'm not the leopard anymore, and I can't hear Spade talking. My stomach lurches, and colors blur and spin.

I know exactly what's happening. I've felt this sensation many times, though never when my consciousness has been in a Skin that's so far away from my physical body.

My consciousness is transferring back to my human self.

The person who's taken over President Morelle's Skin must have just wiped my chip.

TWENTY-TWO

President Morelle is bending over me.

I stare at her for a moment, then sit up in my pod. Her complexion is as flawless as ever, and her silky hair barely moves as she straightens. She's holding the scanner she used to wipe my chip, and her piercing eyes stay fixed on me as I detach myself from the various tubes that were feeding me and taking away my waste.

I wince and mutter curses as I pull the tubes out, but President Morelle says nothing.

The person using the Skin is waiting to see if I know who they are. If I've figured it out.

Once I'm free, I drag in a deep breath, ordering my heart to stop skipping in my chest, and my hands to stop sweating.

"Hello, Sentin." I make my tone as calm as I can.

President Morelle smiles. Sentin rarely shows emotion, but I can tell he's pleased I know it's him.

"Hello, Milla." His voice sounds like Morelle, just like mine did when I used that Skin.

"You're not dead," I say flatly.

"When did you start to suspect I wasn't?"

I pull myself out of the pod to stand on my own two legs. My body feels stiff and sore, and I've got small cuts all over me. Superficial damage, like the wounds suffered by my Leopard Skin. The expensive medical equipment hooked up to the pod was probably already in the process of healing me.

"Not until I saw you on the holo just now," I tell him. "Until then, I was mourning you. I really thought you were dead." A surge of anger floods through me, and my tone becomes bitter. "I cried for you."

Morelle cocks her head just like Sentin used to do in his Reptile Skin. "I'm sorry for putting you through that. Though I must admit to feeling glad that you missed me."

I put a hand on the pod to steady myself. After all this time using the President's Skin, and then my Leopard Skin, it feels odd to be in my own human body again. The pod has been keeping my muscles exercised and my body healthy, but my legs feel wobbly because they haven't been used for so long, and I could do with a shower.

"You had Morelle's scientists make you a Skin, didn't you?" I ask. "The idea did occur to me, but you know what convinced me you were human? That cut on your hand you got from Felicity's window. It didn't heal nearly as quickly as my Skin does."

"When I first cut myself, I was in my human body, and I replicated the wound on the Skin, which was grown from my own DNA. I resisted the urge to have the scientists strengthen the Skin, or use any synthetic materials or specialized nanites in its manufacture. It was identical to my own body in every way. It even smelled like me, didn't it?" He sounds pleased with himself.

"You planned to blow yourself up?" I ask.

"The imperator was a difficult man. He would never have negotiated in good faith, no matter what we offered. Prince Otho needed to take the throne if we were to have any chance of peace, and the only way to achieve that was to remove his father."

"Why didn't you tell me what you were planning?"

The door to the hidden room is open, and I can see out into the library. Sentin's human body is nowhere in sight, of course. He wouldn't leave it where it could be found. He's much too smart for that.

"If I'd told you, Prince Otho would never have believed you were innocent of his father's murder. You're not that good a liar."

I take in a deep, slow breath, fighting to keep my emotions as firmly under control as his always are. Until now, I would have given anything to bring Sentin back from the dead. But now I know the truth, his betrayal stings.

"You always planned to take the President's Skin for yourself, didn't you?" I'm relieved my voice doesn't give away my anger.

"Of course. Thank you for taking on the role until I was ready for it."

I clench my teeth. "All this time, I've never known you to be sarcastic."

"Sarcastic?" President Morelle gives one of Sentin's slow blinks. "Not at all. I'm truly grateful for the part you played. It was necessary for me to stay in my human body to get us into Deiterra, but I don't need that body anymore. You've done an admirable job, and have become an impressive leader. But now it's time for me to take full control in order to lead Triton through our upcoming unification with Deiterra."

I pinch my lips together for a moment, and when I'm

sure I can keep my tone calm, I ask, "Did you arrange for the Beast to kill Felicity?"

His gaze drops and he shakes his head. "I hope you can believe me when I tell you that wasn't part of the plan. I didn't think he'd take it that far. For what it's worth, I'm sorry." He sounds sincere, but it's hard to believe him. Cogs are whirring in my head as I put together everything that's happened. It all worked out to his advantage, and I'm pretty sure he planned it that way, manipulating me and everyone else so we did exactly what he wanted.

"So let me guess," I say. "You're the one who suggested to the scientists that they should upgrade my Leopard Skin. You wanted the Beast gone and decided I should kill him for you. And you knew that while I was doing that, I'd leave President Morelle's Skin here for you to transfer into. I practically gift-wrapped it for you."

"I merely guided you in the direction Triton needed to go. We're steering both Triton and Deiterra into a better future, and Kriston Welcon and his kind can't be part of that. I'm sure you and I agree on that?"

"When your Skin was killed in Deiterra, you transferred your consciousness back to your human body in Triton. Then you stayed in hiding until I came back and took out the Beast for you." I have to force my teeth not to clench. How easy I must have been to manipulate. All this time, I've been dancing to his tune.

"Don't feel upset for doing the things you've done. Edward Morelle thought you were unpredictable, but I've come to know you better than he did. The one thing I could count on is that you never flinch from doing what you perceive is the right thing. You and Cale are alike that way." He chuckles. "But you surprised me when you transferred ownership of the Morelle factories to the Fist. It's fortunate

I didn't delay becoming President Morelle any longer. Thankfully, I still have time to reverse the transfer."

I let go of the pod and stalk to the door, moving stiffly. "In Deiterra I asked you what kind of future you're creating, and you never answered me. Will you tell me now?"

He follows me through the library. "I've already made it clear that I want a unified land. Triton and Deiterra need to become one."

"One country, with you at the wheel. You want power over it all." I lead him into the hallway, heading toward the living room.

"Only the strongest leader can forge a path to take a billion people into a better future."

"Will your version of the future mean more misery for Old Triton?"

"Change must occur slowly to avoid disruption. But eventually, Old Triton will benefit."

"Slow change won't help the people who are suffering now." I reach the middle of the living room and stop, turning to face him. "You know what I think? One person shouldn't have this much power, no matter how smart they are."

President Morelle's face is impassive. "Deiterra and Triton will be safe in my hands. Now the Beast is dead, I'll take control of his factories. Once the consortium is gone and I run all the factories in Old Triton, I'll improve conditions globally, rather than piecemeal, the way you attempted to do."

The stiffness is slowly leaving my body. I flex my muscles, pumping more blood into them and testing how they feel. My human body is still strong. And thanks to my recent use of my improved Leopard Skin, I might have grown even stronger.

I doubt I could win a fight against Sentin now he's using President Morelle's Skin, but I need to do something. He's not the only one with an idea of what the future should be like, and in my version, President Morelle doesn't become dictator-for-life, or let Old Triton suffer.

"What about me?" I ask.

"You could work with me," he suggests. "You're resourceful and clever. I counted on you to negotiate the peace treaty with Otho, and you didn't let me down."

I grit my teeth, forcing myself not to say something I'll regret. He wants me to work with him after tricking me into thinking he was dead? Not going to happen.

But I need to keep him talking, to give Keren and Spade more time. I'm not entirely sure they'll do what I asked them to, and even if they step up, it'll take them a while.

"Lay it out for me," I suggest, walking to the large feature window in the living room, and gazing out at both Triton and Deiterra. "Tell me everything you have planned. Help me see what you see."

I force my gaze to stay up, so I keep looking out at the Deiterran wall and the green fields beyond it instead of dropping my eyes. Felicity fell from this window, and the image is all too fresh in my mind. I don't want to glance down at the ground far below.

Sentin joins me at the window, standing beside me. He wobbles a little in President Morelle's trademark high-heeled shoes. It took me a while to get used to them too.

"Triton's technology will transform the Deiterran landscape," he says. "While their land is becoming more productive to feed a greater population, some New Tritoners will find ways to cross the wall. The elite will go first, searching for a lifestyle they can't have here in Triton, with the means to buy or influence their way into a land that will remain officially off-limits for many years."

"And then?"

"As more people settle on Deiterran lands, the Deiterran economy will prosper, and population pressures in Triton will eventually ease."

"In New Triton, you mean?"

"To begin with. I know you're concerned about the people of Old Triton, but without their efforts, Triton's economy would grind to a halt. We can improve their conditions, but stability will require an active working class. That will only change once the factories are fully automated, and a new social structure is in place."

Sentin speaks for some time, laying out his plans. I listen with only half my attention, trying to estimate how long it might take Keren and Spade to do what I asked.

"What if something happened to all the factories?" I ask when he stops talking. "Say they were all destroyed. What then?"

Sentin frowns. "Hypothetically speaking?"

"If there were no factories, what would it mean for New Triton? Walk me through it."

As he spells out the terrible consequences, I keep asking questions. Having his plans succeed has made Sentin more talkative than usual, but I doubt it'll last much longer.

Sure enough, he eventually checks the time on his band. "I have other things to attend to," he says. "Before I go, I need to know whether you've decided to work with me or against me."

He stares fixedly out at Deiterra while he waits for my answer, as though he's worried I'll be able to tell what he's thinking if he meets my gaze. It almost seems like he's holding his breath, although I don't know why he wants me on his side. President Morelle is only a little taller than I am, and her frame is deceptively slight, but I know firsthand how powerful Sentin must be feeling, especially as he stares at the cities and farmland he plans to rule.

"What if I think what you're doing is wrong?" I ask.

He lets out a breath. "In that case, I would ask you to leave the building, and our paths are unlikely to cross again. But I expect you could find a home with your mother, now that she has one."

"You wouldn't try to kill me?"

"I see no benefit in that." He frowns at me. "Is that your answer? Will you insist we need to be enemies?"

I put my hand on the window, feeling the coldness of the pane. "I need to tell you something." I let out a long breath. "I did something that's going to mess up all your plans."

"What's that?"

"Down there." I point to the Deiterran wall. "I asked the Fist to transport the Beast's cache of explosives to the wall and blow it up."

"You what?" I've never heard Sentin sound more startled. He frowns, his eyes raking the length of the wall, searching for movement.

When it comes, the explosion sounds like a long rumble rather than a bang. It's quieter than I expected, perhaps because we're a long way up and the sound is muffled. As the rumble starts, a cloud of dust rises from the wall, blocking our view of what might be happening beneath it. The floor moves under my feet, the enormous scraper swaying.

Sentin draws in a sharp breath, bringing both hands up to the glass. His attention is totally focused on what's going on outside. He doesn't see me move behind him.

As the dust billows higher and the rumbling grows louder, I gather all my strength and shove him as hard as I can into the window.

Sentin doesn't know that when this pane of glass was replaced, I told them to use normal glass instead of the extra thick, bullet-proof stuff he had installed in the rest of the windows.

The glass shatters and we both fall through it.

TWENTY-THREE

For a panicked moment, I'm falling just like Felicity did, and pure, icy-cold terror floods my brain, wiping out all thought.

Then I grab for the edge of the window. Broken glass slices into my hands, but I manage to close my fingers around the window frame. Hanging below the window, I dangle in the howling wind.

Below me, President Morelle falls.

If I wasn't so strong, there's no way I wouldn't fall too. As it is, it takes every bit of my strength to haul myself back inside. Long before I manage to struggle to my feet in the living room, the president has disappeared far below, lost in the dust and smoke that's still billowing from the Deiterran wall.

Wincing, I pick slivers of glass from my hands, then strip the cover from one of the couch cushions and press my palms into it to soak up the blood.

There's no time to clean myself up any more than that. I need to get out of here.

In the elevator on the way down to the ground floor, I

realize I'm trembling. Sentin must have opened his eyes in his human body by now. Just like me, he must be flesh and blood again.

My Leopard Skin is probably still in the Phoenix Industries building, in the place I was standing when Sentin wiped my chip. I have no way to transfer into it anymore, and no scanner to recode my chip. Besides, President Morelle already announced a total ban on Skins. I imagine the stompers will collect it, and destroy it. The thought is terrible, but I feel numb, like too much is happening too fast for reality to sink in.

The wall has come down.

Even though I'm the one who planned the destruction of the wall, I can't believe it's happened. I took a guess at what might happen to Triton without it, but there's no way to know. I doubt even Sentin could predict what might come next.

When I get to the ground floor, I walk quickly away from the Morelle scraper, keeping my head down and using the stolen cushion cover to hide my bloody hands and the fact I have no band.

A small crowd is gathering at the side of the scraper, where the president's body must have landed. After a fall from that height, there won't be much left of her. She'll probably only be identified by the band that was on her wrist, and I doubt anyone will be able to tell she was a Skin and not a real person.

More people are heading toward where the dust and smoke are still rising, and I join them, trying to mingle with them though they're New Tritoners and I don't look like them. Still, I make it away from the scraper without being stopped.

The bullets that take passengers down to Old Triton are

jammed full, with lines of people waiting to board. Even the long twenty-eight-floor stairwell is packed, but eventually I make it down to Deiterra, forcing my way through the crowd. It seems like everyone in Triton wants to see what's going on for themselves.

The closer I get to the Deiterran wall, the thicker the smoke and dust become. It's gritty in my throat, and so dense that many of the people I'm walking with give up. They turn back to where the air is clearer, presumably to watch and re-watch footage of the explosion on their bands.

I pull my T-shirt up over my nose and mouth and keep going, though my eyes are streaming and I'm coughing into my shirt. I don't stop until I'm in front of the rubble that used to be the Deiterran wall.

A figure emerges from the gloom and stops in front of me.

"Hey," says Cale, his voice muffled by the cloth he's wrapped around his nose and mouth.

"Hey yourself."

He steps forward to wrap me in his arms, and I bury my face in his shoulder. Through the cloth over my nose, I catch a sharp chemical smell on his clothes. The same scent that was in the Beast's weapons room.

We stand like that for a very long time, holding each other without talking while the smoke and dust gradually settle.

As the air gets slowly fresher, more people start emerging from the darkness of Old Triton, gaping at what's happened to the wall.

I twist in Cale's arms so I can see it for myself, and he lets me go. He fumbles for my hand, but I wince and draw it away.

"You're hurt," he says.

"Only scratches."

His brow creases and though I can only see his worried eyes above the cloth still wrapped around his face, I can tell he wants to make a big deal of my bloody hands.

"Come on," I say, picking my way toward the still-hazy pile of rubble. "Let's take a look."

Somebody brushes past me, a woman who's hurrying toward the wall. More people are behind her. Cale and I join the flow, clambering over rocks and giant chunks of concrete. Cale sticks close beside me, and we both see it at the same moment. His intake of breath is audible through the cloth over his mouth.

So much of the wall has come down, the fields of Deiterra are clearly visible beyond it, and Old Tritoners are starting to pour through the ruins, scrambling over the rubble and climbing down into the open space beyond. From our vantage point, I can see some have already reached the giant trees and are staring up into their branches, or reaching out to touch their trunks.

Cale and I follow them, finally getting clear of the smoke and dust as we cross to the other side. With more and more people passing us from behind, it feels like a flood rushing into Deiterra. The sun is hot and bright like it is in New Triton, highlighting the dirty grey clothes and sallow skins of the sinkers around us.

Cale pulls the cloth off his face. "They're going to eat the Deiterrans' food and trample on their crops."

With my own face exposed, I drag in a deep breath of fresh air. "It'll be chaos for a while, but we'll have to find a way to co-exist without a wall."

In front of us, in the shade of one of the giant trees, an old woman is swaying as though she's going to fall over. Tears are cutting tracks through the dirt on her face.

"Are you okay?" Cale takes her arm.

The woman's face is weathered and her hands are twisted claws. Broken veins spread thin red lines over her cheeks. She reeks of street brew. A rough sleeper, no doubt, and my guess is her body won't hold out much longer.

She blinks at Cale, then turns her filmy, bloodshot eyes to me. "It's so beautiful." Her hoarse voice is barely louder than a whisper. "Has this always been here?"

"It has, Gama," I tell her gently.

"If I'd known..." She doesn't say what she might have done, but sinks to the ground and tugs a bottle of street brew out of her coat. She offers it to us, but we shake our heads.

Cale and I leave her sitting under the tree, and walk a little further, drawn to the rows of plants as though we're seeing them for the first time.

"What happens now?" he asks.

I run one of my uninjured fingers over the top of a leaf. "Old Tritoners will have a choice to make. Stay in Triton, or take their chances in Deiterra."

"I don't think Deiterra is ready for an huge influx of people."

"The stockpiles of food we found in the Beast's building will help for a while, and I bet we can find more stockpiles in the buildings of his cronies. There are five more industrialists in the consortium. It's about time they shared their supplies."

Cale is silent for a while. He's running his own fingers over the tops of the plants, staring intently down at them as though they can give him all the answers he needs.

"What about the factories?" he asks.

"The Fist owns all of President Morelle's factories now. They'll need to offer good wages to attract workers. And so will the other factory owners."

He shakes his head, looking back at the Old Tritoners still pouring through the gap in the wall. "Otho isn't going to like this."

"We'll help him handle it. Tori's with him, and she's resourceful. And that intensive farming you were talking about? We need to get it working."

"There's a lot to do."

I nod. "We'll need to all pull together and help. You and me, the Fist, Otho, Tori, and everyone else we can recruit. The wall is gone now, and we can't put it back. We have no choice but to make this work."

"You know what?" he says slowly. "I think we can do it. Not that it'll be easy, but we can find a way." His gaze meets mine and in the sunlight, his eyes look pure gold. They're tiger's eyes.

My heart lifts, and I smile back at him. "Of course we can. We'll do it together."

Stepping forward, he runs his hand over my cheek. I barely notice when his fingers brush my scars. All I can think of is how warm his eyes are, and how much I've missed the feel of his lips on mine.

And when his face bends to mine, I can think of nothing at all.

EPILOGUE

"We'll have vegetables," says Ma. "With creamy potatoes."

Fussing in the kitchen of her new house, she looks so happy, it makes my heart feel light.

"Not stew?" I make a show of slumping in my chair at the dining table, pretending to be disappointed. "I really wanted stew."

"Vegetables," she repeats, her smile getting wider. "I want the freshest I can lay my hands on for tomorrow night. Have you tasted vegetables from Deiterra? I might be able to get some at the market. Never mind the expense, this is a special occasion."

I exchange a glance with Cale, who's sitting beside me.

"Has William actually said he's coming?" Cale asks carefully.

"I spoke to him yesterday, and he promised." Ma brings a pitcher of sweet tea to the table and pours us all a glass. Her grey hair is neatly trimmed in a new style, and she looks a lot less exhausted than she used to. She has a smudge of white powder on her cheek from whatever cake is currently in the oven, producing such a delicious smell.

Since moving into her small one-bedroom apartment in New Triton, Ma's cooked so much food, it would take us months to eat it all. And still, she keeps up filling up more storage containers. Pretty soon we'll need to start giving food away.

And as tiny as it is, she's filled her apartment with plants, until there's barely enough room to move around. Pots line every windowsill, their leaves embracing the New Triton sun. The aromas that drift from the herbs in her kitchen compete with her cooking smells in the best possible way. No wonder she looks so happy here.

"Does William know Cale and I are coming for dinner tomorrow?" I ask.

"Of course, love. I told him."

"And he still said he'd turn up?"

"Seven o'clock sharp."

"Okay." I pick up the cold glass in front of me and take a sip. Ma makes the best tea. It has just the right amount of sweetness. Just like Ma herself, who's determined not to let William and me stay angry with each other. And all her cajoling and bullying is working. William and I aren't friends yet, but maybe one of these days we'll surprise ourselves.

"The tea is delicious." Cale taps his band, checking the time. "But I'm afraid we can't stay long. We asked Keren to meet us here. We're going to a meeting—" He's cut off by a knock at the door. "That must be her now."

When he opens the door, Keren comes in. She looks more drawn and tired every time I see her, but I guess that's to be expected. She and the other Fist members have been working hard, trying to cope with all the changes. I don't envy her the job of running the Morelle Corporation, but she's been handling it as well as can be expected.

"I'll see you tomorrow night, Ma." I kiss her cheek and give her a hug. She hugs me back fiercely, as though she's not going to see me again for months, though I make sure to visit her at least three times a week.

Then Cale, Keren and I head out to the elevators. As we ride down to the ground floor, Keren turns to us with a serious expression. "Did you see the latest news?" She activates her holo and a face appears above her band.

It's Sentin. He's not wearing his glasses, and his angular face looks darker than it used to. His hair is slicked back, and he's wearing a suit.

"Times have changed," he says in his slow, New Triton accent. "We must change too. A vote for me is a vote for a united future."

A woman's voice speaks from off-camera. "You were late announcing your candidacy. Why do you think you've become so popular in such a short amount of time?"

Sentin appears to ponder the question for a moment. Then he says, "People still remember that I won the Skin Hunter Contest. They know I was instrumental in negotiating the peace treaty with the Deiterran imperator that ended the war and saved thousands of innocent lives. They understand that I can continue to navigate our changing relationship with Deiterra. And they trust me to succeed when it comes to steering the future direction of Triton."

"You're campaigning on the promise of a more tightly controlled border, giving only selected entrants the opportunity to move to Deiterra."

He inclines his head. "The current border controls have been instrumental in stabilizing the economies of both Triton and Deiterra. However, they don't go far enough. Stricter borders will ensure the long-term prosperity of both

Deiterra and Triton. The imperator and I are in mutual agreement on that point."

"I have one last question," says the woman. "And it's an odd one, but I think you've seen the persistent rumor that keeps cropping up on the feed. Will you address it once and for all?"

"You're talking about the gossip regarding my apparent suicide while in Deiterra?" Sentin chuckles. "Reports of my death were greatly exaggerated."

Keren flicks the holo display off, and we step out into the brightness of a New Triton day. "He's only just announced he's running, and he's already leading the polls," she says.

She must have called a cab, because it's waiting for us outside Ma's building. As we approach, its door opens. We pile inside, Cale and I sitting next to each other, with Keren facing us.

As the cab glides smoothly into traffic, I say what I'm sure we're all thinking. "Sentin will be elected."

Cale nods. "I think we can count on it."

"Should we be worried?" asks Keren.

Cale looks at me, his eyebrows raised, waiting for my opinion.

"I'm not sure." I admit. "Maybe. But Sentin did tell me he wanted what was best for Triton and Deiterra. I believe he really is trying to make the world a better place, at least as he sees it."

"How can you be certain he was telling the truth?" Cale asks. "After everything he did, and what happened to Felicity, doesn't it seem like he just wanted as much power as he could get?"

"I guess we're about to find out. In a few weeks he'll be president of Triton."

"I wish you'd run for the job," mutters Keren. "You'd have a real shot at beating him. Everyone listens to you."

I give her a weary look. We've had this conversation a dozen times, and I'm not going to change my mind. "Maybe it's a good thing Sentin's going to be president." I tell her. "At least he'll keep us on our toes."

"It definitely won't be boring," Cale agrees with a laugh.

"We could do with the excitement," I add, just because I love the way his eyes sparkle when he's amused.

Keren lets out a huff of breath, shaking her head at us. "Will you two stop it? And Milla, are you going to talk to Tori today?"

"Don't I always?" Tori's still in Deiterra with Otho, but now we've expanded the network, it's easy enough for us to talk everyday. It's not like we're short of things to discuss. They've had their problems with the influx of Tritoners pouring over the border, but things are settling down now the flood's turned into a trickle, and Old Tritoners are showing the Deiterrans how hard they're used to working. It's been a crazy few months, but hints of equilibrium are starting to appear.

"Is their water supply still running low?" asks Cale.

Keren frowns. "Can you ship them desalinated water from the coast?"

"We can, and we will." That's my answer for most things, and it's working so far. The Fist doesn't have a single leader anymore, but Cale and I are on the committee. We both took responsibility for fixing a wide variety of problems, and we're slowly managing to work everything out.

I lift my hand to my face, scratching my hollow cheek though my scars don't itch nearly as much as they used to. Most days I forget they're there at all.

Sometimes I need to remind myself that I'm just Milla.

I'm still stronger than most, but otherwise I'm a regular person. Once I felt vulnerable all the time. Now, I can handle anything. Especially when Cale looks at me like he's doing right now.

The cab gets to the bullet, slows a little to connect with the track, then plunges down to Old Triton. Shadows close over us as we descend, but our cab's interior lights brighten, making the cramped space seem cosy rather than gloomy.

Old Triton's still dark, but other things have changed. The streets aren't crowded anymore, or as dangerous as they used to be. There are no rough sleepers. The shelters barely house the limited numbers they were designed for, because wages are high enough that many workers have moved to apartments instead.

The ex-knights I charged to make Old Triton safer did just that. Once out of their Knight Skins, they remembered they were human. Sure, there were a few exceptions. But mostly, they did even better than I'd hoped.

"You ready for another busy day at work?" Cale asks as the cab pulls up outside the factory. He takes my hand and squeezes it with a smile that warms my heart.

The factory looks very different compared to what it used to be like when I worked on the line, sweating over the super-heated machines. Among other things, I'm running this factory now, and I'm trying to make it the best workplace it can be. Decent pay, higher safety standards, and no more double shifts. And that's just the start of what I have planned.

I smile back at Cale, then lean in for a kiss.

"Another long day at the factory?" I ask softly. "Believe it or not, I'm looking forward to it."

And amazingly enough, it's true.

AFTERWORD

Dear Wonderful Reader,

Thank you for reading the Skin Hunter trilogy. I hope you enjoyed it. These books have been a labor of love, and I'm thrilled to have been able to share them with you.

If you'd like to read more books set in Triton and Deit-erra, please let me know. You can contact me through my website (www.taniahutley.com). While you're there, please join my VIP Club so you get emailed about future releases.

And if you like the way I tell a story, you may enjoy the urban fantasy series I'm co-writing with a friend. You can join the VIP Club to hear more about that series too.

Thanks again for reading the Skin Hunter series. I appreciate your support, and look forward to sharing more stories with you in the future.

- Tania.